Charles King

The Colonel's Christmas Dinner

Charles King

The Colonel's Christmas Dinner

ISBN/EAN: 9783743385221

Manufactured in Europe, USA, Canada, Australia, Japa

Cover: Foto ©Andreas Hilbeck / pixelio.de

Manufactured and distributed by brebook publishing software (www.brebook.com)

Charles King

The Colonel's Christmas Dinner

THE
COLONEL'S CHRISTMAS DINNER.

EDITED BY

CAPT. CHARLES KING,

U. S. ARMY.

PHILADELPHIA:

L. R. HAMERSLY & CO.,

1510 CHESTNUT STREET.

1890.

THE COLONEL'S CHRISTMAS DINNER.

INTRODUCTION.

At sunset on the 24th of December the commanding officer of Fort Blank was mentally as blue as the trousers of his pet orderly and facially black as the self-same orderly's boots—minus the shine. The north mail was just in, borne by a half-breed Sioux on a more than half-starved pony, and thereby came the news that three officials high in repute and moderately so in rank in their respective corps would arrive late on the following day and spend the night at the post. They had been far to the northward, "investigating" at the Agencies along the Wakpa Washtay, and had not even found a reason for the misnomer. Everybody who was ever there believes that the water of that fabled stream was good only when skillfully diluted. They had started for the distant railway, hoping to reach their domestic friends by Christmas Day. But bad luck befell them. A gale and blinding snow-storm swept over the northwest from Boulder to the Black Hills. Their driver lost the way—first—and the mules next. The party camped in a cañon " until the clouds rolled by "—were found and towed into an outlying cantonment by a scouting band of troopers, and now, here they were "coming to roost in my rookery," said the Colonel, "when I haven't even a crow to pick with them."

But this was not the sum total of his troubles. There was worse news—or lack of news, which meant bad news in this case—from the south. He had planned a quiet little dinner—just half-a-dozen of his cronies and favorites, and indeed there was but scanty room for more—the invitations had been issued and accepted ; his worthy helpmate and their eldest daughter were already deep in preparation : when lo !—the fact he had to face on Christmas Eve was that Christmas Day was apt to bring him double-loaded tribulation. The same storm that brought him extra guests had blocked the coming of the extra dinner.

Fort Blank's market-town lay just about a hundred miles away, when the skies and roads were clear, and just about a thousand when they weren't. The oysters, the turkeys, the celery, the cranberries, the fruits ordered sent by the stage due at Blank at 4 P.M. on the 24th, were stuck in the snow-drifts an indefinite distance south. Even the telegraph couldn't find them.

When a man's in trouble, in nine cases out of ten, the quicker he tells his wife, the sooner it's over. The Colonel went home overcome with the weight of his woe. For a moment his better half was, apparently, as prostrated as himself—no woman likes to have a dinner-party ruined, either by having too little to eat or too many to eat it— but no sooner did she note his profound dejection, than she arose to the occasion.

"Never mind, Colonel, the missing dinner will turn up in time, and if it doesn't, we'll make them so welcome, after their hard trip, that anything will taste good. And then, you know, there's the champagne we were saving for Dot's wedding. It will cover a multitude of sins— like charity. Don't you worry. I'll manage it."

And she did.

That woman was a marvel of energy, pluck, and

resources. She trotted over through the gloaming to her especial crony, the Major's kindly wife, catching the children peeping over the balusters ready to scream with ecstasy at the sight of a possible Santa Claus.

She had brief consultation with her. She hurried down the line to the bachelor dens and pounced on Mr. Briggs, who, though devoted to "Dot," was as yet understood to be on terms of probation. There wasn't anything Briggs wouldn't do for her—now, at least—and Briggs, before tattoo, was riding away through the glistening moonlight over the rolling expanse of snow "scouting for that dinner" with an all-night jaunt before him. She had roused the sympathies of the garrison. Strangers are coming—all unexpected—but must be welcomed.

It is a characteristic of frontier life that the very men and women who entertain and express at times most unflattering opinions of their neighbors, from the "C. O." down to the "Sub," will turn to, when the honor of the garrison is at stake, and help them out to the extent of their spoons, salad forks, their most treasured china—their last cent, and Fort Blank rallied to a woman to the support of the Colonel and his energetic wife.

All through the crisp, sparkling sheen of the moonlit evening, dark, muffled forms were flitting from house to house along the lines of officers' quarters. Little packages of gifts—home-made, perhaps, but loving—were left for the children everywhere, and then there was perpetual stamping of overshoes on the Colonel's porch and laughing greetings of party after party that came trooping in—everybody bringing material aid and comfort.

And so before midnight the modest little dinner originally proposed developed into a phenomenal "spread." Even by tight squeezing, which the jolly subalterns advocated, not more than ten people could be seated in the frontier dining-room, but "hang the dining-room!" said the Major. "Set a long table down this side of the house —one end in the dining-room—t'other in the parlor. Knock out the folding doors, of course—levy on all the flags, curtains—Navajo blankets, lap robes, crazy quilts and Indian shawls and their imitations in garrison. Call in the combined resources of the bachelors' mess and private establishments—and I'll bet you will make such a dazzling table of it that even if we haven't turkey and quail enough to go round they won't notice it. Then just fall to and decide how many of us you want to appear, and we'll turn out in our best bib and tucker and the old house will fairly sparkle."

The Colonel's wife sprang up and seized the speaker's hands. "Just what I hoped for, only—we'll have to borrow so much."

"Borrow anything we've got, and I'll throw in more than a gallon of that old Amontillado of mine to boot."

"*Major!* That precious sherry? You are simply too generous!"

"Not a bit! I'll be here to help drink it and I'd love to see their faces as they sip it."

The Major's wife would have embraced him then and there, but time was precious. His enthusiasm was contagious, and this was the result. The bachelors' mess contributed *nem. con.* two dozen plump quail from their larder and enough celery to make "salad for sixty." Captain and Mrs. Winston begged that they might be represented by half-a-dozen bottles of some prized Chateau Yquem they had stored away for special occasions. The Waynes trotted out some dusty flagons of Pape Clément which the Captain had laid away when serving in New Orleans. McManus, the jovial post trader, appeared with a brace of bottles of his "warranted twenty years old S.

O. P., Currnel—and ivery limon, fig, nut, raisin or dhrop there is in the house." Fluids were after all the hardest things to provide for: that is to say, fluids of suitable quality, and yet this was galore.

"By Jove!" said the Colonel, "This isn't my dinner. It's the whole post that's doing it." But no! said the post. "It's the Colonel's Christmas dinner, and we are only too glad to help."

And lo! What transformation scene was wrought by Christmas afternoon. Briggs had found the stage thirty miles out and had replaced its battered team by the well-fed mules he had taken along. By noon its precious cargo was landed at the Colonel's kitchen, where half-a-dozen ladies were at work. Mrs. Waring had assumed charge of the cake and pastry department. Captain Wayne's accomplished wife was up to her lovely elbows in flour. The Adjutant's better half was out in the snow superintending the manufacture of orange ice and chocolate cream (a whole box of McManus's Floridas was squeezed into those freezers and "divil a cint would he iver take "). The Q. M. Department had knocked up a temporary kitchen in the back-yard, where a big range was already firing up, and haunches of "black tail" and a saddle of venison were hanging in the frosty air ready for their turn. Over at Mrs. Morton's the soup had been simmering ever since tattoo the night before—two troopers from the "Grays" on watch over it lest the fire get too hot or too low.

Nobody could beat the Quartermaster's wife in the preparation of coffee—that was to be her province when the time came. And as for delicious jelly, there was bonny Mrs. Prime, the Doctor's wife, with him away till the stage got in, and then it was too late for him to prohibit the expenditure of certain hospital stores which he

afterwards very gladly replaced from personal funds. And
so all was bustle without, and willing hands had been as
busy within the improvised banquet hall. Extra tables,
chairs, china, glasses of all shapes, styles and colors,
decanters, carafes, sconces, candelabra, damask, cutlery,
silver, etc., had been poured in as fast as needed. Nobody had to be asked for anything, everybody sent hi—
no! her best. At 3 P. M., under a canopy consisting of
the great garrison flag, draped from the front of the
parlor to the rear of the dining-room, with all manner of
smaller flags, guidons, signal outfits, and improvised
drapery too intricate for description, the Colonel's Christmas table was laid for twenty-four, and was a sight that
set his eyes glistening to match the array of crystal. No
flowers, of course, for 'twas in the heart of the Rockies
and the dead of winter. No wax tapers, for there wasn't
time to provide them, but in their stead, from scores of
brilliant (tin) sconces, from candlesticks, candelabra,
clusters by the dozen, there popped out the prim white
"best adamantine" of the Commissary Department.
"Bless your heart! Mrs. Grace," said the A. A. C. S.:
"They'll make just as soft a light as wax, if there isn't a
draft, and just as brilliant if you burn enough at a time."

At four thirty the lookouts reported the ambulance
toiling over the divide five miles away. "Here they
come!" was the cry. "Now everybody who is to be at
the dinner scatter and dress. I close the banquet hall
against all comers until it's time to light up," ordered the
Colonel's wife, "and mind—be here sharp at six. They'll
be ravenous by the time they reach the post."

"Stop! stop! my dear—one minute!" shouted the
Colonel from across the hall. "Just listen to this." And
with twinkling eyes the veteran read aloud a little note
he held in a hand that trembled despite himself.

"DEAR COLONEL GRACE :

"All day I have been lamenting that there was nothing I could do to show my interest in the dinner you are giving to our unexpected guests. The stage came in the nick of time. It brought me from New York my special favorites of the club days a few years ago. With my best wishes for the Merriest of Christmases to all I send this box of Regalia Perfectos.

Yours most ——"

But he couldn't finish.

"Pills junior—God bless him !" shouted the Major, "and I've been doing nothing but guy him since he joined ——"

"*Colonel !*" screamed Mrs. Grace. "And we hadn't room for him."

"Make it, by Jove ! Raise the roof ! Why, there wasn't a cigar worth smoking on the post—and, damn these medical chaps anyway, they—they——"

"They do the nicest things in the nicest way," prompted Mrs. Grace. "Doctor Watts comes if I have to stand."

"Nonsense ! Two more seats can go in there just as well as not," declared Miss Dot. "I would *like* to squeeze the doctor if you will put him next me."

"Dora ! you are excited," remarked mamma. "We'll have the doctor here—next Mrs. Willis. You are to devote yourself to Major Loomis. But that'll make twenty-three. We must match him. Now, which—who ?"

"I'll run right over and tell her—Kitty, of course," and Miss Dora makes a dash. In vain Mrs. Grace would have interposed. The Colonel settles it.

Kitty Wallace, by all means, or *he* wouldn't care to come. Now, I've just time to go over and hug Pills myself."

*　　*　　*　　*　　*　　*　　*　　*　　*

Fancy the astonishment of those three hungry and weary travelers, Colonels C—— and D—— and Major

I,——, when, as they were assisted, stiff and half-frozen, from the ambulance and marshaled aloft to warm and cosy rooms, they were told that dinner would be ready as soon as they were, and a few friends to meet them. "Wear what you like," said the Colonel. "We know you have only traveling garb."

But as they thawed out under the influence of the genial glow, the abundant hot water, the sounds and, it must be added, the scents from below, for a big dinner announces itself all over the army quarters of those days before ever the grace is said, the three gentlemen realized something, at least, of what was in store for them.

"Fatigue uniform is the best we can do," said Major Loomis. "I can see shoulder knots and aiguillettes gathering below."

"Fatigue it is," was the prompt response, and then there came a sudden flock of dancing lights along the roadway in front, the tramp of martial footsteps. "The band, by Jove!" said the Major, and the band it was, for an instant after there burst upon the frosty air the ringing, joyous notes of a welcoming quickstep, only one tune, for the valves of the clarionettes would freeze stiff in less than no time. But to that spirited music, marshaled by their host, they descended upon a hall full of "fair women and brave men" in all the gala of social dress.

"Dinner is served," announced the one colored factotum at the post, throwing open the door at the head of the hall. Mrs. Grace stole her gloved hand within the arm of Colonel C——, and before that distinguished soldier had had time to bow to three people he was being led down a banqueting board, the like of which he had never seen or dreamed of seeing on the frontier in all his years of gallant service. Speedily the guests were marshaled to their places—every one seemed to know just where to go. There was an instant of reverent silence as the voice of the old chaplain quavered its thanks and its plea for blessing on one and all. Then a rustle and subdued clatter, hushed voices for a while as the party exchanged nods and smiles and stole covert glances at the three storm-worn travelers as though seeking to read in their bearded faces what they thought of the unusual display. Colonel C——'s twinkling eyes were taking in the pretty scene with frank and genial delight. Anybody could tell from *her* smiles and heightened color that he was saying to Mrs. Grace just the loveliest possible things of the beautiful effect of the table—and well he might. Under the bright-hued drapery the glare of the candles was skillfully toned by countless tiny screens of pink tissue paper on wire frames. (Didn't three of those blessed women spend hours in cutting, pasting and trimming them?) The "adamantines" on the table were all similarly dressed with little pink bells, so that nowhere was there flame in sight. Yet the light was amply strong to bring out all the beauties of the board—the lovely costumes of the women, their own charming faces, the rich variety in the appointments of the table, in crystal, in china, in cut-glass. "Who on earth," said old Colonel D——, before he had been seated a moment, "would have dared dream of such a sight as this? Blue Points on the half-shell in the heart of the Rockies!"

They were not Blue Points—neither were they shells. They were bound to utilize those oysters (canned "selects") somehow, and this was an inspiration of the Adjutant. At each place as the banqueters took their seats stood a little block of clearest ice, six inches square and two deep, hollowed out on the upper surface, and therein reposed five of the smallest oysters that could be selected from the "selects." It was fun to see that energetic of-

ficial spending hours that afternoon with the piccolo
player and the bass drummer, sawing out those "shells"
from the huge blocks duly dumped in the back-yard and
then laboriously hollowing out the top of each by the in-
genious application of hot shot—a couple of stray twelve-
pounder howitzer shells that, long since emptied and un-
fused, had been kicking about the post since the memory
of the oldest log in the block-house at the angle.

And while these metamorphosed "selects" were being
tipped with lemon juice and horse radish and slipped
down past welcoming palates, white-gloved, solemn-faced
"strikers"—the Major's eagle eye upon them—were filling the tiny sherry glasses (and half-filling those of
larger calibre) with his treasured Amontillado. A well-
drilled corps they proved—these extemporized Jeameses—
for while everything was being brought in from the door
at Mrs. Grace's end of the double room—everything went
out at the other.

"By Jove—what sherry!" exclaimed old D——. He
was too far away from the Colonel to be heard by
him, but Mrs. Grace smiled her pleasure at his satisfaction and her eyes signaled "fill up again." Out went
the ice blocks. In came two huge tureens of fragrant
mock turtle and these were deposited on little stands on
each side of the table, where the plates were quickly
filled and set before the guests. "Capital idea that! Mrs.
Grace," said D—— again. "By Jove, madam, you must
permit me to compliment you on such management. It
would be sure to cool if carried in plates from the kitchen,
and if there's anything hateful it's cold soup. Especially
when one has been exposed to storm and tempest and
zero weather for a week in the mountains as we have.
More sherry? Indeed, yes. I'll lose no time in drinking
your health."

And Mrs. Grace smilingly raised her glass and bowed her acknowledgments and just glanced at the humorous twinkle in the blue eyes of Colonel C——, who sat at the right hand, and who promptly sipped a ripple from the surface of his sherry as token of his sympathy in the toast.

And now the chat grew merry and general. Down the table far to the right, handsome young Doctor Watts was beaming into the blushing face of Kitty Wallace. Midway on the other side, sprightly "Dot" was "doing her level best" to fascinate dark-visaged Major Loomis, as bidden—while Briggs, whose heroic efforts had been rewarded by a seat at her other side, was scowling at the situation and reaching for more sherry. It was McManus's "best" that lay at his elbow, for the Colonel meant to use his Major's Amontillado on Sam Ward's principle—a thimble-full, and all who struck for more (except among the guests from abroad) should take the local product. A lovely woman, a visitor at the fort, was making play with her beautiful blue eyes at bluff Colonel D——, who took her in; but he was too full of his recent hardships to care for comforts less material than those to be found in his immediate front. Midway down the table the staunch ally of Mrs. Grace—the Major's wife—finding Briggs moody, decided on striving to console him, but at this moment the blue-eyed dame, finding old D—— intractable and being unaccustomed to anything less than rapt attention, took advantage of an instant's turn of Major Loomis's head, and he was caught. "Dot," rejoicing in her release from duty, turned to whisper to Briggs. Smiles, social sunshine, joyousness reigned along the board, and the Major's wife, happy in such consummation of their hopes, sent a significant look along over the wine glasses and through the pink tissue candle-bells to her

loyal friend and social chief at the head of the table, and
Mrs. Grace caught it behind her fan and smiled back as
the great haunch of venison came in.

At her right, beyond the senior officer of all—the low-
voiced gentleman in the quiet fatigue dress—sat pretty
Mrs. Wayne exchanging congratulations with the
aiguilletted Adjutant who was just beyond. Then there
was Mrs. Winston, wife of the soldierly, scholarly senior
Captain, who sat far down at the Colonel's end chatting
with Mrs. Quartermaster Drake over the trials and tri-
umphs of the day. Then there was the Captain whose
life was said to have been a romance, and the woman who
had not had too much of anything but reality, and who
could serenely and sweetly enjoy so bright a scene as this,
even though her thoughts were much with the little ones
at her modest fireside who had begged for some of the
goodies when she came home (I wish you could have
seen the load that the Colonel helped her to carry to those
sleeping cherubs, when we broke up—never mind at what
hour). And the Colonel had taken in the bride—the wife
of the Post Surgeon who wouldn't have been able to get
here at all, but for Briggs and his mules. And the gray-
haired chaplain and his wife were there and the quartermaster, of course, and you may be sure old McManus,
the jovial trader, was bidden, but he wouldn't come.
"Lord! Currnel, I'd be like a fish out o' wather, and
then, d'ye mind, it's the boys are all coming to the shtore
to-night for the bit of spread I'm givin' them." And so
what did the Graces and their counsellors do, but send
and insist his pretty daughter should come, the apple of
the old man's "oi," and nothing could have rejoiced him
more.

By the time the turkeys were gone—wild and domestic—people were well filled, and still there came another

course, the quails of the bachelor mess, with such marvelous celery salad! And old D—— had waxed eloquent over the sauterne and exploded with amaze at sight of Pape Clément in Wyoming, and wouldn't be admonished by the disapproving glance bent upon him by his senior across the table, and burst out with "But, madam, this is magic. This beats Aladdin; beats—beats anything I ever heard of—*beats the Jews!* You couldn't have known we were coming more n a day and you couldn't have done better if you'd known it a year. Now I never heard of Pape Clément outside of New Orleans before. Why! I couldn't have been more surprised if you had given us Pompano——"

Pop! went a champagne cork, just under his rubicund nose. He buried his grizzled moustache in the hissing fluid—Dot's wedding wine—and glanced about him a picture of bliss, defiant of adverse comment or criticism.

And now, fun, laughter, witty sallies, jovial anecdotes were criss-crossing over the board. The huge plum pudding, all wealth and blue blazes, was borne aloft by the sable functionary down the long length of the room, and there, by aid of comrade hands, placed in front of the Colonel, whose face was as roseate and blissful as D——'s, and round as the pudding's. Pop! pop! the champagne corks went flying. Dot's wedding wine was to be taxed, only enough to season the birds. Then again 'twas Mc-Manus *ad libitum.* And everybody praised the pudding, though few could eat it, and the health of the fair manufacturer was drunk, and the Adjutant's wife came in for a general toast on her ices and cream, and McManus's fruits were heaped before unheeding eyes, and at last came Mrs. Drake's masterpiece—coffee so black and rich that it left a stain on the dainty china in which it was served, and then the Colonel arose, and people at his end of the **table**

stopped talking, and little by little the silence spread.
"Fill your glasses," he said. "Soldiers, soldiers' wives—
and—soldiers' wives that ought to be."

"Bravo !" from D——.

"Oh ! I forget you, Dot," said the Colonel, amidst
shouts of laughter and applause, but glasses were filled,
and then as the old fellow raised his on high a sudden
hush fell upon them all.

"We don't often have such a chance as this, my friends.
I've no words to say what joy it gives my heart to welcome you all here at this God-given and blessed season of
cheer and gladness. I've no words appropriate to the
Christmas-tide, dearly though I love it, but I bid you
join with me in drinking—one and all—the toast that at
all times, at all seasons, wherever under God's provi-
dence we may be called to serve, must ever be first and
foremost in the American heart : The President—and the
Flag !"

Bang ! went a gong somewhere out in the hallway, and
as all sprang to their feet there broke upon the still night
air without, in full swing, the crash of the band, joined
almost instantly by a score of manly voices, "ould
McManus" leading the stirring strains of "The Star-
Spangled Banner." It was the climax of the evening.
They had been rehearsing an hour "down at the store."

"And now," said the Colonel half an hour later, by
which time the enthusiasm had subsided to some degree,
"Our Guests" and "The Ladies" had been appropri-
ately toasted and responded for (the former doubly so, as
after Colonel C—— had spoken his few modest, well-chosen
words D—— sprang to his feet and waxed exuberant).

"And now," said Grace, "we have talked over our little
programme, the ladies and I. There's nothing for them
to do, if banished. They are all indulgent as to the mat-

ter of good tobacco smoke. They have made this little dinner—every bit of it—the success our indulgent friends have pronounced it, and it would break my heart if they were to leave." ("Break all our hearts!" shouts from everywhere). "I read not long ago of a Christmas at Sea, where the ward-room officers entertained the Admiral and their Captain and, over the walnuts and wine, told their stories each in turn.

"In almost every respect they had manifest advantages over us fellows. But in one, which outrivals theirs combined, we have the best of 'em. They had no ladies and, thank God! we have, and the best and dearest and truest in the whole Army, if I do say it. (Deafening applause).

"They have willed—and who dare disobey?—that each man here, when summoned, shall so contribute his share to the enjoyment of our Christmas night. I have done my share of the talk" ("No!—No!"), "and my duties are now at an end. It is the high privilege of the host to encourage his guests by leading off with the first story, but it is the still more blessed right of the regimental commander to transfer his burden to the shoulders of his staff. In the exercise of that right, I call upon my Adjutant for the first story. Mr. X., take the floor."

Amidst long-continued applause the gallant old soldier took his seat, and then, one by one, regretfully, the guests turned to the other end of the table, where sat Mr. X. blushing over his aiguillettes.

THE ADJUTANT'S STORY.

"Well," said the Adjutant, "if somebody must start the ball, I will try, though yarn-spinning isn't my forte, and I shall break down utterly if I see signs of satirical comment anywhere."

"Oh, shut your eyes and tell it as 'Pills' does when he sings for us," suggested the Senior Lieutenant, always ready to have a fling at the Adjutant.

"Yes, and when I open them again find the room deserted, as he did the night you got him to sing at Mrs. Freeman's." At this there was a general shout of laughter, for the incident was still fresh in the memory of the garrison.

"No," continued the Adjutant, "I'll try and tell the story. It all happened the winter my old troop was stationed at Fort Emory, and if you don't believe in ghosts you can ridicule it as much as you like."

"A ghost story!" exclaimed the lady with the blue eyes. "Oh, that's delightful! But we ought to have the room darkened." There was no response to this suggestion, however, and the Adjutant went on.

"It was a mighty hard winter. It had been blowing and snowing much of December, and by the time the holidays came on, the whole country seemed buried under the drifts. We were penned up in the post, for, unless there was imminent need, nobody wanted to send out teams in such weather. The mail was carried over to the railway twice a week by Indians who made the trip in two or three days by using up several ponies. Otherwise we had had no communication with the settlements since the twelfth of the month. Now that winter Jim Forbes and I were living together. He was serving with 'F' troop, and I with 'K.' We had the set of quarters at the lower end of the row, nearest the stables and farthest from the commanding officer's. Colonel Hawes, of the —th Foot, was in command. His family was with him— his wife, three children and a distant connection of his wife's, Miss Frazier, a fragile, delicate girl of about twenty, who had no home of her own, it seems, and who, by being governess, and heaven knows what all besides to those three youngsters, managed to eke out a living and have a home under the Colonel's roof

"She was a shy, retiring sort of a girl, with big brown eyes; something awfully pathetic about them, I thought at times; but I never saw anything of her when we called at the Colonel's, and on pleasant days when she was out walking with the children she avoided notice in every way, and seemed positively scared if any of us bowed or spoke to her. She came out with Mrs. Hawes and the children late in the fall, and the winter set in soon and put a stop to her out-door pleasures, if she had any, and then Forbes took to calling frequently at the Colonel's by night, and to taking notice to those graceless kids by day. As he had hardly been on cordial terms with the family before, it was evident there was some new attraction.

"I was very fond of Jim. He was a big, burly fellow, rough as a miner and soft-hearted as a woman——"

"As a major, I thought you were going to say," put in Mr. Briggs.

"Do be quiet, Mr. Briggs," pouted the Major's wife. The Colonel frowned, and glancing around the table, Briggs found that people were getting interested and that perhaps he had better subside. The Adjutant took advantage of the diversion to imbibe a little Dutch courage from his champagne glass, and then went on:

"I say I was fond of Forbes. He was not a brilliant fellow, like Briggs here, but he was stanch and true; a good son and brother, as I had reason to know while his mother was alive; but he was practically alone in the world now, and rather solemn at times. He had one pronounced fad. Without being a spiritualist, he somehow believed in spirits. He used to sit in a big, easy rocking-chair on his side of our centre-table nights when we were alone and tell me about his mother and how often he saw her and talked with her now. I told him it was all dreaming ; but he believed in it, and used to wax really eloquent, talking about his theories by the hour. We had an open fireplace, and burned hickory logs then, and though it was only a bachelor ranch, we were pretty snug and comfortable. Night after night, as the winter came on and the wind howled about the old shell of a shanty, we sat there in front of the roaring blaze, he with his pipe, and always rocking to and fro, to and fro as he talked, and I got to know him better and like him better every day.

" ' Why,' said he one night, ' you laugh at my thinking I can hear mother moving around my bed, or sometimes bending over to kiss me as she used to when I was a boy. Now we've been pretty close friends here for a couple of years, old man ; don't you suppose that if I were to die I'd want to come back and see how you were getting along without me ? Why, it would be just as natural for me to come drifting in some night and setting this old chair of mine to rocking, and communing with you just as I do now. I don't suppose I'd be visible to you ; but it seems as though I could make my presence known. I'll tell you what : If I'm killed or suddenly taken away any time while you are here, and my theory is all right, that our souls can rustle around on earth awhile, I'll let you know I'm gone in that way. I'll just float in here and start my old rocker going.'

" Of course I simply laughed at him ; but there came a night when I didn't.

" I didn't care to go often to the Colonel's ; he was very prosy, and would talk for hours on regulations and papers, but Forbes got to going up there two and three and then four nights a week. Mrs. Hawes was quick enough to divine the attraction, and as she hoped with another year to live in a city and educate her brood at some fashionable school, she doubtless thought it a good plan to marry off Miss Frazier, and Forbes would make a capital husband. He was just the man a woman could rule with a look. And so Miss Frazier was brought down from the upper regions and made to sing and play for him, which she did not at all want to do as it turned out : and, as she was being obviously thrown at his head, the result was inevitable : she began to hate the sight of him; and big honest Jim used to come home looking bluer and bluer, and sighing like a dozen furnaces, and yet saying no word. I got nervous about it, and was for getting somebody to go and steer Mrs. Hawes onto the other tack, when old Boreas himself took a hand and helped us in a most unexpected way.

"Jim had been in the depths of despond for a whole week. It had been snowing night and day, when on the evening of the 19th, I think it was, he came back from the Colonel's earlier than ever.

"'Where can I get a sleigh?' he asked.

"'I don't know, Jim, unless the trader has one. Why?' And then he told me. Miss Frazier had a brother, an only brother, it seems, who was far from strong, and who had grievously offended his aunt, Mrs. Hawes, a year or two before. Miss Frazier's heart was bound up in the young fellow, and she had received a letter saying that at last he had obtained a good appointment in southern California where the physicians had urged his going ; that he must be in San Francisco on the first of January ; but that he was coming around by the way of the old K. P., and they would spend Christmas eve together. He could not go on to the fort, for he would not set foot under the Hawes's roof. She must come in to Grover City, the nearest railway town where there was a good hotel. With the cheerful ignorance of all men who have never been West, he thought it a perfectly feasible thing to drive over the intervening forty miles at any time ; and now there was not a trail that wasn't deep in snow. The Colonel and his wife had coldly told her the trip was simply impossible and bade her telegraph to him to hire a sleigh and strong team and come out to the fort. In such weather and for such a trip it would cost a fabulous sum, and her brother had not a surplus cent. She was sobbing aloft in her little room while Mrs. Hawes was dilating to Forbes upon the utter absurdity of the whole thing. ' It's nothing but an absurd sentiment on her part. Of course if there were any way of bringing them together I would do it. But there isn't. The Colonel says no horses or mules could possibly make the trip. She's just crying herself sick over it.'

" Then what does Forbes do but scribble a note and send it to her by one of her pupils, saying in so many words that he would either get her to town or fetch her brother out to the fort, but at taps he was back in the house again with a face as long as my story. There wasn't a thing on runners in the post. The nearest sleigh that he could hear of was at Rayburn's ranch, ten miles over on the Saline At dawn he rode away, permission being rather grudgingly granted, we thought ; took an Arrapahoe guide with him and two horses, and then we heard nothing more until late in the evening, when he drove in with a really good sleigh, but a played out team. He had gone over thirty miles through unbroken drifts to get it.

" Next morning, with two fresh horses, hired of old Grubb, our post trader, he loaded up the sleigh with

robes and rations, and was away at daybreak bound for
Grover City; and though I didn't feel like talking with
Mrs. Hawes, I did want to see Miss Frazier, and tell her
how blithely Jim had started. He expected to drive
slowly all day long, with frequent rests and plenty of feed
for the team, and to reach Murray's ranch at night,
twenty miles away. After that he would find at least
partially broken roads and could get along faster. It was
a glorious, sunshiny winter's day. The snow sparkled
and glistened. The sun was so warm that the eaves
began to drip, and the women and children came flocking
out on the porches, snow-balling from house to house.
The Colonel had ordered out a party to follow the telegraph line and locate the breaks, and I was really sorry
the detail had fallen to another fellow and not to me, as I
walked up to the Colonel's and asked for Miss Frazier.
She looked even more fragile than ever when she came
into the parlor from the school-room. Her big eyes were
full of anxiety and longing, and heavy tear-drops began
to gather the moment I told her of Jim's buoyant start at
dawn. She knew of his going—her window commanded
a view of what had been the road for several miles—and
yet, instead of being glad and hopeful, as I supposed, she
was profoundly depressed. 'I cannot help it,' she said,
throwing herself into a chair. 'I have been haunted by
most dreadful dreams; tormented by all manner of fore-
bodings. Oh, I wish he had not gone!'

"Now this was not at all what I had expected or hoped
for, but I tried to cheer her; told her Jim would find
rapidly clearing roads, and would have her brother at our
house before sundown on the 24th, possibly by noon.
'And Mr. Frazier's room is all ready for him,' I added;
'and we'll have a jolly Christmas dinner there. Mrs.
Stannard is coming to see you this morning. She will

matronize the party, for it was arranged weeks ago that she and Captain Stannard were to be our Christmas guests. Then the next day we will see Mr. Frazier safely over to the railway and off for 'Frisco.' And still she was sad and unresponsive. I could not rouse her at all. I went and got Mrs. Stannard to run over and see her. And that night I went again. Mrs. Stannard said she feared Miss Frazier would be ill, she was in such distress of mind. 'She cannot sleep without being tortured by dreams in which she sees Mr. Forbes and her brother lost on the prairie and freezing to death in some terrible storm. She cannot close her eyes without the picture rising before her at the instant.' Now this was the evening of the 21st. The detachment came in and said they had followed the telegraph line for seven miles; that many poles were down and the wires were buried out of sight in a thousand places. They also said that Forbes with his sleigh had followed the line instead of the road. It was straighter, but went up hill and down dale in a way no wagon could follow, and it might be difficult for him.

"On the 22d about nightfall an Indian runner came in with our letter mail. He said Forbes had got to Murray's all right, despite several upsets. So far, so good. There was a letter for Miss Frazier, and I was not surprised to get a message before tattoo. Mrs. Stannard wanted me to come to her a moment.

"Just as I supposed. Miss Frazier was there with her brother's letter, and the poor girl was well-nigh heart-broken. He had been seized with a hemorrhage at St. Louis, and forbidden to start at the time proposed. He could now reach Grover City only by noon of the 23d, and it might be the last time, he said, that he could ever hope to see her loved face. It was now arranged that for a little change and rest she should remain with Mrs.

Stannard a day or two. The dreams that so terrified her might not pursue her there.

"But they did. When I went over to inquire the next day, the poor girl was nearly wild. 'Is there no way, no way to stop them?' she cried. 'They must not attempt to come. It is death to both.' But we reasoned with her; pointed out how the skies were cloudless; the weather settled; assured her that by this time Frazier and Forbes were probably getting ready to start and would spend the night at Murray's Ranch. She only hid her face and moaned. 'I have brought this upon them,' she cried. 'I have driven them to their death.' And I went off feeling almighty queer, I can tell you.

"Yet the sun went down in cloudless splendor. There wasn't a breath of air stirring. I thought I would run over to Stannard's to get them out to see the sunset, thinking it would cheer them. But the western sky began to turn yellow, not red, and I went back. At tattoo I tramped over to the hospital to read the barometer, hoping to come back and assure her that it said, 'Set Fair.' But I went to the trader's instead and offered Jake Cooley, one of our half-breed scouts, twenty-five dollars to make the night ride to Murray's. He looked surprised, said all right, jumped off the bar where he was sitting and started down to the corral for his broncho; but came back in ten minutes and said he wouldn't try it for fifty. The wind was beginning to moan about the haystacks; and the guard were ordered to get their buffalo coats and overshoes.

"Before dawn the windows were rattling. Still there was nothing really alarming in the weather. But when the morning light came creeping in, the air was full of snow-flakes again and the skies were heavily overcast. I won't go into details. Those of us who were with the regiment that winter will never forget the blizzard that

followed. By noon a gale of seventy-five miles an hour
was raging from the north, a blinding storm of snow from
the sky and drifts from the surface was whirling into the
faces of the few who dared venture forth, and the mercury
had fallen to twenty below zero. It was simply awful.
And not a word of news had we from Forbes or Frazier,
even when nightfall came.

"And now comes the strange part of my story : I had
been over at Stannard's trying hard to think of something
to cheer or comfort that poor girl ; but it was useless.
She was either staggering up and down the room, wring-
ing her hands, or else moaning on the sofa. Mrs. Stannard could do nothing to drive away her awful dread. I
tried to assure her that Forbes was so skilled a plainsman
that he would never think of quitting shelter on so threatening a morning. But she shook her head. 'I know him
—I know him. He will only think of the promise he
made me,' was her reply. At tattoo I left them and the
wind blew me down the line and past my own gate and
would have whirled me to the stables if I hadn't grabbed
the fence. All sentries had been drawn inside. There
was no attempt to form companies for roll-call. Everybody was indoors. A blazing fire was roaring in our
chimney place as I entered : but I confess I was utterly depressed, the girl's foreboding had so affected
me. It was useless to attempt rescue of any kind.
All was dark as Erebus on the howling prairie, and
neither man nor beast could make his way northward
against that storm. I threw myself in my old padded arm-
chair and drew it close to the hearth ; but the blast roared
in the chimney and fairly shook the house from roof to cellar, rattling the blinds and sashes and driving the snow
through every crevice. Even our old cat and her frolic-
some kittens seemed uneasy and worried, and Tabby,

who never so honored me when Jim was home, sprang
into my lap for petting and comfort that I was too heavy-
hearted to give; and so with querulous 'miaow' she
went back to her brood in the basket. And there I sat,
pretty well worn out, I can tell you, with distress and
anxiety, thinking despite myself of all Forbes had ever
said of coming back from the spirit world and rocking
here in his old chair. There it stood, looking so lone-
some, empty, silent, that I half turned as though to
stretch out my hand and give it a sympathetic pat, but I
could not reach it; it was full five feet away. And just
then,—how he managed to blow in that storm, I don't
know,—but some one of the infantry buglers up at the
north end of the parade got out on the covered veranda
and began to sound taps. Never in my life had I heard
it like that: so wild, so weird, and so despairing. Many
a time it had wailed 'put out your light' over the grave
of some poor fellow whom we had buried in Arizona or
under the shadows of the mountains; but never did it
sound to me as it did that awful night, and for the life of
me I could not help thinking of her dream and of Jim's
strange promise to me. I felt a cold chill running all over
me, and I huddled closer to the fire as the last note died
away, completely ready now to believe with her that it
was their requiem. And then,—then if I had needed
something to banish the last lingering doubt, it came. Believe me or not as you choose, but as true as I sit here
and tell this story,—as true as I live and breathe,—just
as the last note of taps died away, without a sound, without a touch from any source that I could see, without the
faintest reason—Forbes' big rocking-chair settled suddenly
back as though he had lowered himself into it, and then
rocked violently to and fro.

"No, I didn't faint or cry out or run. I just fell back in

my own chair with every hair standing on end, chilled to
the marrow.   I lay back there glaring at that awful chair
as it slowly ceased its rocking ; and at last I got up,
reached the dining-room somehow, swallowed a glass of
whiskey and was striving to get back some vestige of
nerve when the front door burst open and a big burly man
plunged in.   'Help me get him out of the saddle!
We're both frozen,' he cried,—and it was my blessed old
Jim still in the flesh.   I yelled for our striker, and in a
moment more the three of us, between us, had lugged in
a fur-covered stranger, too exhausted to speak.   The
horses fled to the stables down under the hill.   The
striker ran for Stannard and the doctor, and in five minutes Helen Frazier, wild-eyed, tearful, but rejoicing beyond all words, was kneeling by her brother's side.

" 'I'll be all right soon,' he whispered at last.   'I'm
not frozen.   Look to the lieutenant!   He made me wear
his fur gloves and buffalo shoes.'   And then we found Jim
had vanished to the kitchen, and there he was ankle deep
in a tub of snow, while Bell, the striker, was plunging
his master's blue-white fingers into a bucket similarly
filled.

" And yet, with of course this exception," proceeded
the Adjutant after a pause, " our Christmas dinner the
next day was the most delightful I ever knew.   As though
to make amends for its fury of the day before, the weather
was simply perfect.   Most of us went to morning service
in our little chapel, and almost everybody came in to see
Jim and pat him on the back, for his hands and feet were
all done up in bandages; and over again Mr. Frazier
smilingly had to tell of that fearful trip from Murray's
ranch.   The wind being at their backs they had thought
to get along all right, but soon after starting the snow got
so thick, the gale so violent and the drifts so deep that

they were capsized again and again, and at last the pole snapped short off. They abandoned the sleigh, and Forbes had hauled his fur gloves and overshoes on his companion's resisting hands and feet, for Frazier was utterly unprepared for such an outing. Then Jim lifted the young fellow on the off horse, mounted the near one himself, and so they were simply blown along for fifteen miles. Again and again the horses fell in the drifts and Forbes would pick Frazier up, set him back and then on they would plunge, blinded, breathless, almost exhausted and frozen stiff, when at last the poor brutes landed them within the shelter of the garrison.

"Well, that evening we had our Christmas dinner, Mrs. Stannard presiding at one end of the table, Stannard and I doing the carving for the crowd; for we had in the chaplain and his wife and two daughters and two of the bachelor officers, Mr. and Miss Frazier and Jim. Just a dozen, though Forbes could not sit at the table. He was bolstered up in that imp of a rocking-chair, with his bandaged feet on another, yet jolly and happy as he could be, for Miss Frazier cut up his turkey for him, and the way she blushed made her look pretty as a picture. And —that about ends it. I got a seven days' leave, and Frazier and I made the trip to Grover City all right; and when I came back at the end of the week and went over to the Colonel's with a package Frazier gave me for his sister, little Kitty Hawes showed me right into the parlor, and there were Jim and Miss Frazier sitting side by side on the sofa, and would you believe it? instead of being glad to see me when she jumped up, she ran right out of the room, and was still red as a rose when Jim at last coaxed her back. She is Mrs. Captain Forbes, of the quartermaster's department now, and a mighty sweet woman too. And her brother gained health and money both, at San Diego, and—d,— well, as I said, that's about all there was to it."

"But, Mr. X.," exclaimed two or three feminine voices at once, "you haven't accounted for that chair's behaving so. I never heard anything so weird and mysterious in all my life."

"Now do you know," said the Adjutant, "that thing puzzled me for a whole week after I got back. I wouldn't tell Jim about it. It impressed me so strangely. And now that he was spending all his evenings at the Colonel's I wouldn't sit alone with the confounded chair. It gave me cold shivers to look at it, and I used to clear out and go calling, or down to the store, and one night I had to be in for a minute, and all of a sudden, just as it did the night of the gale, just as taps were sounding, too, that infernal—I beg your pardon—that blessed chair suddenly began to rock again. Why, you ought to have seen me start for the door. I grabbed my cap, flew around the table, and then there was a fearful, blood-curdling yell."

"Oh, Mr. X.," shuddered the Colonel's daughter.

"Yes, a fearful, blood-curdling yell, I give you my word. You see I stepped square on to the liveliest of the kittens, just after the little brute had pitched off the hind end of that rocker. Its weight was enough to tilt back the chair and set it going."

For a moment there was a dead silence. People looked at one another, and then the sentiment of the entire table, doubtless, was voiced by the lady with the sweet blue eyes.

"Mr. X., I declare I think you're a fraud."

The Adjutant having scored a dead failure, it seemed difficult for the moment to find a successor. Briggs was called for, but begged off on the plea that if *that* was a specimen of the light-weights' work, it was time to call on the seniors.

" Not a bit of it," boomed the Major in his ponderous basso. " We want to give you boys your day now—early in the battle, when people are not sleepy and eager to go home, as they may be after hearing you talk."

" I appeal from the Major to the chair," laughed Briggs, bowing diplomatically to the father of the feast.

" And the chair sustains the Major. Go on, Briggs. Do what you can for the sake of the subs," replied the Colonel.

" It's too much like voting on a court," said the Lieutenant. " I'm glad the ladies are here to do away with the idea that it is a court," and he glanced at the bright face smiling by his side. It gave him courage, at least. " And if I'm to be the next victim, the sooner it's over the better. Here goes——

THE SENIOR LIEUTENANT'S STORY.

" When Jack Talbot was thirty years old and had, after eight years' service, attained the exalted rank of senior second lieutenant of his regiment, he suddenly conceived the idea of taking unto himself a wife. It is hard to say exactly what put this thought into his head, for if there ever was an army bachelor unsuited for matrimony, it was Jack.

" To begin with he was as poor as the proverbial church-mouse, head over heels in debt (the interest he paid would have supported a poor family), very extravagant, and with about as much idea of economy or business as a babe—and then again he had become so wedded to his bachelor ways of life, that any radical change seemed fraught with a great deal of danger. Jack himself never appreciated these things—in fact he had an idea that he was

2*

just the man to make a most proper and excellent head of
a family. 'Of course I'll have to make a great many personal sacrifices,' he mused to himself as the idea began to
grow on him ; 'no more card practice—no more staying
out late at nights—no more fast horses—no more—in fact,
no more foolishness,' and Jack pulled himself together
with a sudden virtuous determination that was delightful
to behold ; on the other hand, however, he continued, 'Instead of the aimless, shiftless existence I've been leading for
some years, there'll be something to live for—some one to
work for—some one to brighten and cheer my quarters,
and best of all, some one to sympathize with me when
I've had a row with "Old Graball," who, by the way, was
the regimental quartermaster, and the only man in the
regiment that John detested, and with whom he was continually skirmishing. Now when a man decides to marry,
there is generally some one in his mind's eye ; but with
Jack this was not at all the case. In fact, this important
feature seemed to have escaped him entirely, and he only
thought of the future Mrs. Talbot in a general hazy sort
of a way. 'Now there'll be no false sentiments about
this,' he confided to his particular friend, Dick Abbey, the
first lieutenant of his company. 'I intend to make this
purely a matter of business. In the first place I shall select
some nice, sensible, well-bred girl, who can pay her own
mess bill, state the case to her exactly, show to her the
mutual advantages of such a combination, and—presto !
the thing is done. Then we'll settle down to a quiet,
home-like life, live economically, pay my debts, and become
the best of friends in the world. No, sir,' continued Jack,
becoming quite animated with his theme, 'no mawkish
sentiments for me ; given good hard common sense, mutual respect and confidence, and the result is marital
happiness.'

"There was an amused smile on Dick Abbey's handsome face, as, after listening to Jack's homily, be said : ' But, old man suppose the girl says no ? ' 'Oh, come now— she'll hardly say that, you know ; marriage is the ultimatum, or rather the mission of all women,' Jack continued ; ' there are plenty of just the kind of girls I've described to you—that would be glad of the opportunity. Of course,' he continued, as Dick was about to reply—' of course I know what you are going to say— that marriage without love means unhappiness, or affectionate toleration, at the most ; but really, old man, I think you're entirely wrong ; who is it that says, "Even perfect love cannot last more than six years" ? Can six years of even ideal love repay for years and years of vain regret after the awakening has come, after all illusions have been dispelled, and after the glamour has faded and worn away. Nay, nay, my good Dick, prate me not of woman's love.' And Jack looked at his companion with an air of triumph, that reminded one strongly of Joe Willet after one of his celebrated arguments.

' "Well, old fellow, I wish you luck,' Dick said after some little silence ; 'you know you have my very best wishes, but I would advise you to consider the matter very carefully before taking any action ' And declining Jack's hospitable offer of a toddy, he bade him a hearty good-night, and left. For some time after his departure Jack sat silently smoking an imported cigar (one of the sacrifices *in futurum*) and busily engaged with the absorbing idea that had lately taken complete possession of him. Clearly his thoughts were of the pleasantest, for his face generally assumed a happy, contented expression until it fairly beamed, and, unable any longer to restrain himself, he burst forth into :

'Where art thou now, my beloved '—

with (I must confess it) more ardor than harmony.

" This was an unfortunate proceeding on his part however, for it aroused old Graball, who lived across the hall, and who, as soon as he heard Jack singing, came to his door and proceeded to give a very successful imitation of a dog howling in great pain.

" For some time the harmonious blending of the voices was kept up, until the absurdity of the situation striking Jack, he ceased singing and burst into a roar of laughter, much to the Quartermaster's distrust and surprise, who thereupon incontinently fled.

" Peace having been once more restored, the matrimonially disposed warrior donned his cap and cape and proceeded leisurely to the club to give the fellows one more chance before he left forever the charmed but wicked circle of army bachelors. It was a gala night at the club ; somebody was having a birthday, and Talbot's appearance was hailed with cheers and cries of a hearty welcome.

" All the bachelors were there and a few of the married men whose wives were temporarily sojourning in the East. The affair was highly successful—all bumpers and no heel-taps was the rule—and jollity and good fellowship reigned supreme. It is hard to particularize at this late date all that occurred ; it was even a moderately difficult thing to do the next day ; but the great event of the evening was a song by Captain O'Kelley, which was somewhat interrupted by the actions of the junior Lieutenant of the regiment, who insisted on shaking hands with the Captain after every line or two, and a speech made somewhat later on by Talbot, entitled ' Matrimony in the army,' in which he strongly advocated the marriage of all officers, irrespective of rank.

" His little effort was well received by all present except a few of the married officers and the irrepressible junior, who, immediately upon its close, rose somewhat unsteadily to his feet, and with glowing eyes and dishevelled air and manner desired to know if the eloquent orator intended anything personal in his remarks. Having been assured to the contrary, he gravely shook hands with Talbot and disappeared from view, under the table where he contentedly remained until the party broke up in the wee sma' hours of the morning.

"The next morning, in conformity with his new resolutions, Talbot omitted the customary cocktail or bracer, and after the completion of his morning duties proceeded to lay out the plans of his matrimonial campaign.

"Unfortunately for him, there was a scarcity of eligible material in the garrison; in fact, to be precise, there were only two unmarried girls present—one the sister-in-law of Captain Dalton, temporarily visiting him, and, as she informed everybody, 'from the East.'

"One requisite of Talbot's she possessed, viz., money —she had money, and, rumor said, lots of it—but then, poor girl, she needed it.

"A charming thing about our hero was his great love of justice or equity, as he called it, and therefore Miss Manon was duly entered on 'his list,' with probable amount of fortune, and traits and characteristics duly added.

"'LIST OF ELIGIBLES.'

"'No. 1, Miss Dalton, &c.,' &c., and then the list ended.

"The other garrison girl was practically out of the question—that is, from a matrimonial point of view.

"'Dear winsome little Bessie Rawson.' And Jack thought of her with a sigh—if *she* only had the wherewith; but it was not to be thought of, and even if she had the

money, there was her father, 'Old Rawson,' to consider,
a Captain in the regiment, and one of the worst old repro-
bates in it.

"Bessie was only nineteen, and Jack had known her
during his entire service in the regiment; he had watched
her develop from a shy, awkward girl into as dainty and
pure a little woman as ever graced the sex; and then she
was so pretty, and withal seemed so thoroughly unconscious of the fact.

"As a child she had always been devoted to him, and as
they were in the same company, Mr. Talbot soon grew to
be Mr. Jack, a custom still rigidly adhered to.

"'No, it won't do,' he exclaimed after some little
thought, 'it won't do at all; but then, as she is the only
other young girl in the garrison, I'll put her down just to
see how it looks.' So down he jotted 'No. 2, Bessie
Rawson,' and then quite absent-mindedly added, 'No
money, but a fortune in herself.'

"Having exhausted the garrison eligibles, Jack considered the advisability of adding some of the girls he
knew way back in the States; but before he could do so,
there came a sharp knock at the door, and following it
the head of the irrepressible junior, with the invitation
'Come up and see my new fox terrier, Jack; he's a bird;
were going to have a christening' and without waiting
for a reply, slammed the door and rushed back to his
quarters.

"A new dog—that was enough for Jack, and, dropping
the list, he started in pursuit of the lucky owner of the
fox terrier.

"Now the desk at which he had been writing was nearly
in line with one of the windows of his room, and the day
being an exceptionally fine one for November, the
window had been left open.

" An hour or two later, when Jack came back, the list had disappeared.

*   *   *   *   *   *   *   *   *   *

" Whether the disappearance of the list had anything to do with it, it is hard to say, but the truth is that Jack's matrimonial fever abated somewhat during the next week or so.   Not that he had given up the idea; no, indeed; he still preached matrimony to the junior (whenever he could get that doughty warrior to listen to him), and religiously adhered to all his good resolutions.

" November drifted rapidly away, and with December came a cessation of all outside duties, except the absolutely necessary ones, and an increase of gayeties.

" Jack seemed to share a great deal of Miss Manon's time, and it was soon an understood thing (among the ladies at least) that Mr. Talbot was really in earnest, and that an engagement might be expected soon.

" During this period Jack saw little of Bessie Rawson ; she attended the hops and parties, but generally attended by the young bachelor Doctor.

" And what a contrast there was between the girls !

"Miss Manon was always gorgeous, and Jack, who really had an appreciation for the beautiful, would let his eyes wander towards Miss Rawson, charming and restful in the plainest of gowns.

" In order to repay some of their social obligations, the bachelors issued invitations for a swell hop on the 24th of December, and Jack (dreadfully pressed by some of his creditors), after carefully considering all the pros and cons, decided to strike the last blow of his campaign on that night.

" He had no fear of a refusal ; the girl seemed to understand the affair thoroughly ; it certainly was a fair exchange.   Miss Manon wanted a husband and he wanted money, and marriage meant—well, he hardly liked to think what it might mean in the future ; and then there came before him the face of Bessie, with her tender eyes, winsome ways and——

" P'shaw !—p'raps the girl had never given him a serious thought—he was a fool to think of such things—to be sure, they have always been the best of friends and then p'raps after all Miss Manon might say—No, it was not to be thought of. Money—money—he must have it —he would pay off all his debts ; take a long leave ; do the continent, come back to the regiment and then— we'll——

" When Talbot, rather low-spirited and dejected, called for Miss Manon on the night of the 24th, he was positively startled at the girl's appearance ; she was almost pretty in a becoming gown, and there was a look of suppressed excitement on her face that added very materially to it.

" And then the bright, happy manner in which she chatted to him ; it was a revelation. 'By Jove !' thought he, (' she's not so bad after all ;' and by the time they had arrived at the hat-room he was more than half reconciled to his apparent fate.   Of course everybody was there, and looking around the room he caught a glimpse of Bessie Rawson and the Doctor comfortably seated in one of the corners of the room, apparently quite contented.

" She gave him quite the brightest and happiest little smile when she saw him, but before he could get to her she was claimed and whirled out of sight.

" During the entire evening Talbot was restless and ill at ease.

" ' After all, it wasn't such an easy thing to propose to a girl.

" ' Of course, if one loved the woman it would be different ; but then to cold-bloodedly ask a girl to marry you, simply because she had money ; it was a contemptible thing, unmanly, cadish—but in this case quite necessary,' sighed the poor devil, and he waited his chance.

" Just before supper there was an interval of fifteen minutes, and, seizing the opportunity, he asked Miss Manon to take a little stroll out on the porch—' I've something very important to say to you ' he continued, noticing her surprised expression, and together they left the hop-room.

" There were few people outside, and they walked up and down for a few minutes in utter silence.

" Presently Jack said :

" ' Miss Manon—I,' and then came to a dead stop.

" ' Yes, Mr. Talbot ?' encouragingly.

" ' I—Miss Manon, will you be my wife ?'

" ' This is very sudden, Mr. Talbot ;' her voice was wonderfully quiet and contained.

" ' Yes, I know it's sudden ; but then I wanted to ask you for some time. Of course I haven't much to offer you. I'm only a poor Lieutenant in a marching regiment on a small salary, but—but—we've known one another for some time now, and you've grown very dear to me, and I'll try to make you happy,' and egged on by the thought of his unappeased creditors, he warmed up to his work and continued in the same strain for some little time.

" She listened silently to all he had to say, and when she raised her face to his, there was a soft light in her eyes and a sweet, tremulous look about the mouth that argued well in his behalf.

" ' And you do love me ?' she asked

" ' With all my soul,' came his quiet reply, and Jack bent over until his head was suspiciously close to hers.

" Only a moment, and then with a quick gesture the girl drew herself away—' And now take me in, please.'

B2

" ' But your answer ?' he persisted.

" 'Shall be my Christmas gift to you to-morrow,' she replied with a bright smile, and with this he was fain to rest content.

*   *   *   *   *   *   *   *

" For some time after the hop Jack sat in front of the comfortable fire in his quarters smoking and thinking over the night's incidents.

"The girl really loved him and would make him a good wife—that was evident ; and he—well, he liked her fairly well.   To be sure, he hadn't told the exact truth ; but what was a man to say to a woman who asked such embarrassing questions —

" ' And you do love me ?'

" Why, of course he loved her (in a way), and no doubt in a year or so of married life would become quite fond of her, and, humming softly to himself, he put out the lamp and went to bed.

*   *   *   *   *   *   *   *

" The next morning, when Jack came to breakfast at the mess, he found all the fellows there, and lying in front of his plate two envelopes addressed to him.

" He recognized Miss Manon's writing at once—but the other—'why certainly it was Bessie's,' and Jack opened it first.

'GARRISON, Dec. 25th, 18—.

' *My Dear Mr. Jack :*

' Do you remember a promise I made you, when I was a little girl (years ago), that I would tell you of my first proposal? Well, it has come, and I want to be the first to tell you of my engagement to Dr. Roberts.'

" But Jack read no more.

" 'So Bessie Rawson was engaged ? well what of it? wasn't he—or just about to be '—and then he slowly opened the other envelope.

"Great Heavens! what was this? a sheet of weather-stained and soiled paper; he unfolded it almost mechanically, and there he saw staring him in the face the lost 'List of Eligibles,' and beneath it, in Miss Manon's writing: 'It's an ill wind that blows nobody good'—and the bachelors were all surprised when Talbot suddenly exclaimed: ' "Damn the wind'—and left the table, his breakfast untouched."

"A beautiful moral lesson—in one respect at least, Mr. Briggs," was the Colonel's comment, "and I'm glad to learn that manners and morals have both improved in Talbot's regiment since the days of which you tell. Now Captain Rowan, mighty hunter of the —th, people down this end of the table are clamoring to hear from you."

"But I haven't any Christmas story handy," said the tall company commander, a bronzed, soldierly man who looked the stories told of him—that years of his life had been spent scouting, hunting, campaigning from Assiniboia to the Gulf. "I never saw spirits or ghosts, like X. and never knew Briggs' friend Talbot——"

"*I'll* tell you when you saw ghosts—Indian ghosts, Rowan. That was the time you were chased into Wallace. Tell us about that," called Captain Wayne.

"Well—that's something that might happen to anybody," laughed Rowan. "I call it my first experience with

CHILL AND FEVER.

CHILL.

"Probably but a small proportion of those who read of the wonderful sand-storms and mirages of the African deserts are aware that the same, phenomena on almost as large a scale can be seen in our own country. Along the borders of some of the streams of Oklahoma, on the plains of eastern Washington and Oregon, as well as on the Gila desert in Arizona, the sand-dunes change their forms with every passing wind, and the dry and shimmering plains of Kansas and Nebraska, as well as those near Laramie and on the upper course of the Rio Grande, furnish miragic views which astonish and charm the beholder. Wide-spreading lakes tantalize the unsophisticated traveler or hunter ; a buffalo skull with a raven perched upon it becomes a white steed bearing a sable rider ; the coyote sneaking across the field of vision a mile away assumes the proportion of a lion, and, in the days of buffalo, a herd seemed often aerial nondescripts, deriving sustenance from the air in which they were apparently floating.

" Prior to the opening of the Kansas Pacific Railway, and in fact, down to the 70's, the whole of the country lying west of the settlements in Kansas, and along the Platte, swarmed with game of all kinds peculiar to the plains. Officers of the army stationed on the routes in Kansas, could at times count buffalo by thousands, while standing at their doors ; antelope dotted the prairie in all directions, or, gathered in bands of hundreds, in the autumn furnished sport for the hunter, as well as the finest of meat for the soldiers' table. In the timber along some of the streams deer could be found, and among the rocky and storm-worn bluffs bordering other portions of the larger water-courses 'black-tails' or 'mule deer' repaid the toil of the sportsman. There was a spice of danger, too, to give a zest to the sport, and it was not certain that the hunter would not become the hunted, if he ventured far away from his 'base' at the post or camp of the military, or the train of wagons with which he was traveling.

"Fort Wallace was situated on the Smoky Hill Run, about 420 miles west of Kansas City, on the line of the stage-road from that place to Denver, and was for about three years my army home. Directly across the insignificant rivulet called 'the river,' and about two and a half miles from the garrison, the steep bluffs bordering the valley were broken into rough, rocky defiles and cañons, and in them a herd of 'black-tails' had frequently been seen, during the summer and early autumn of '70. No signs of Indians had been discovered near the place for over a year, and, thinking the venture a comparatively safe one, one November morning concluded to 'try for' a deer. My own hunting-pony was not at hand, and I borrowed from the corral one which had been picked up on the prairie some time during the season, and would stand fire without flinching. In fact, he would *stand* anything, and stand it all day, and as for speed, any good train-ox could outrun him, and he was warranted to endure any amount of 'heel-persuasion' his rider had leisure or disposition to bestow upon him. But I had no thought that speed would be required of him that day; and leashing my dog, a powerful and speedy lurcher, I started early for the haunts of the deer.

"The morning was cold, and over the lower grounds along the river a thick fog hid most of the country from view, and I found it yet more dense in the 'breaks' among the bluffs. Still, as I had a favorable wind, and could see a short distance, I carefully picked my way among the rocks, hoping to get a shot at short range. As the sun rose the fog became less opaque, and above it I could see the highest points of the bluffs, when suddenly, from just at the feet of my pony, a jack-rabbit sprang up and hopped leisurely away. The sight was too tempting for the dog's obedience. A plunge or two parted the leash

at his collar, and away went game and hound at racing
speed, up the ravine.   I followed at the best rate of speed
I could get out of the pony over the rocky ground, but by
the time I had gained the head of the gorge, for such it
became before reaching the prairie, the game had time to
have left the country.   A thin haze then hid the face of
the landscape, and I could not trail the dog on the hard
soil.   I was at a loss which direction to take, but rode to
the summit of the nearest swell of ground in the vicinity,
to reconnoiter.   Nothing could be seen of the dog, and I
was turning the pony's head to try another direction,
when I saw something that drove dog and rabbit out of
my thoughts.   My heart gave one bound, and stopped
beating for an instant, and the cold sweat stood out in
bead-like drops on my face, while down my spine ran a
chill that was ice-like in its intensity.   Not more than
a quarter of a mile away, on the next rise of ground, half
a dozen swarthy figures loomed above the fog, and stood out
in bold relief against the horizon, and while I looked
others cantered up.   Then, at a gallop, they started in my
direction.   'How fleet is a glance of the mind!'   I was
at least six miles from the post, on a pony whose best
speed I could almost equal if on foot, if I chose to try the
ravine for shelter.   I might not at once find a place where
they could be descended by my animal, and, once in
them, I was liable to be lost in the fog, only to be found
when it cleared away, with my retreat cut off—if I ran for
home.   I must ride at least three miles before I could get
to a point where my flight could be seen by friends, and
assistance sent.   All this and more went through my
mind like an electric thrill, and whirling the pony sharp-
ly to the left, I plied the 'government brass' in a way
that astonished him, and got all the speed out of him
that was possible.   As I looked back I could see the

heads of my pursuers, rising and falling upon the mist, though apparently not gaining much. Half a mile to the eastward of what I had supposed to be my position when I started, the descent from the high prairie was smooth and easy, and I had directed my course for that point. But I found that I had lost the direction, and was stopped by the perpendicular wall of a branch ravine, which gave no foot-hold for man or beast; so turning squarely to my right, I continued my flight in that direction. As I changed I looked back, but the fog hid my enemy from view. A few hundred yards on I reached the head of the ravine, and turning again to the left, rode in the direction of the garrison. But the pace was telling on my steed, and it was only by constant use of the spur that I could keep him in even a moderate canter. My only hope was that he could hold out till I could reach the brow of the slope, whence smoke of shots could be seen at the post; then shooting him, use his body as a defence, and make the best fight I could, trusting that succor would reach me as soon as possible. By the time he reached it he was down to a walk, and finding a slight 'wash-out,' just at the brow, from which I could see the post, I halted to fight it out. As I faced southward, I found that a slight breeze, before which I had been runing, had dispersed the fog behind me, and my pursuers were nowhere to be seen. While I looked, my dog, following the trail of my horse, came into view where I had struck the ravine, and a few hundred yards in his rear were my pursuers—*a band of eleven antelopes.* The dog, which was nearly white, had killed or lost his game, and, returning to me, had attracted their attention, and, with the curiosity which lures so many of them to their death, they were following him.

"The reaction was in a degree pleasant, but, the tension

gone, I found myself too weak to ride, and man and horse took a good long rest before going on to the fort.

"I said nothing of my stampede, till after I had heard an older officer tell how he was 'scared out of his boots' at the sight of a herd of elk on Laramie plains, thinking them Indian ponies; then I could afford to tell it.

II. FEVER.

"The plains of Western Kansas furnish a rich field for 'the fossil-hunters.' They have in pre-historic ages been the bed of a shallow sea, and in the blue shale, which underlies most of their area, and crops out to the surface in the sides of the wind and rain-swept 'buttes,' the geologist and paleontologist find many rare and valuable specimens. During the years in which I served in that region, several of the first scientists of the country paid visits to the sections lying about Forts Hayes and Wallace, and their discoveries were very valuable. They generally came to the posts provided with letters or orders from Department Commanders, or from the Secretary of War, directing commanding officers to furnish them with such escorts as could be spared, and the duty was one sought after by both officers and enlisted men. 'The professors' were generally genial men, good talkers, and ready to impart information to any one who wished it. One, a naturalist, who looked after the things of the present as well as of the past ages, created a commotion at a dinner table one day, when a small snake, which, for want of a better place to confine it, he had placed in an inside pocket of his 'coat, and covered with his handkerchief, escaped from it to the table, just as the company had seated themselves. The ophidian was harmless as my antelopes, but the stampede was as bad as mine, and the really strange and beautiful 'sarpint' was mashed out of all its proportions by the boot-heel of one of the gentlemen present, before it could be re-captured by its possessor.

"But 'the champion bone-hunter,' as he was designated by the soldiers, was a professor of paleontology from one of the principal eastern colleges, who was accustomed to make extended tours with classes of students of his favorite science, and who, except in the instance about to be related, had no use for any bones which did not antedate Old Father Adam, and the farther back they had existed, the better. Not *wagon*-loads only, but *car*-loads of fossils were found and shipped by him, and he was known to have worked for days, with a pick and spade, unearthing a single specimen.

"His first visit was made the next autumn after the events already related had occurred. With a dozen or more of students, he had spent weeks in the valley of Snake River, in Idaho, and, on his way back to the East, stopped at Fort Wallace, with three or four of his party. His time was limited, but he wished to take a look at the country, and to see a buffalo-hunt, as he had not seen any of the animals in a wild state. They could be found within a few miles of the post, and the morning after his arrival two officers, with about half a dozen mounted soldiers, reported as his escort for the hunt. His party were furnished an ambulance for the trip, and I handed him a rifle and forty rounds of ammunition. The students had their own Winchesters. He expressed his thanks, but said he did not need it, 'had no thoughts of doing any shooting, was only going to look on,' etc., but yielded on being told that no one was allowed to leave the post without being armed. The ground selected was that over which I had been the time before alluded to, as an examination of the rock-formations could be made better

3

there than elsewhere near the post, and the officers took
seats with the party for the time, leading their saddled
horses, while the mounted enlisted men accompanied a
wagon taken along to bring in the beef.   Only a cursory
examination of the rocky defiles was made, the savant
deciding at once that they contained no fossils, and the
party was soon near the head of one of the ravines, from
which egress to the prairie above was practicable for vehi-
cles.   A man, sent ahead to reconnoiter, reported several
small herds on the prairie not far away, and tightening
their pistol-belts, and the 'cinches' of their saddles, the
officers threw their outer coats into the ambulance, and
mounted for the run.   The 'fossil-party' were told that
they could see most of the chase from some rising ground
half a mile ahead, to which the driver was directed to
proceed, and also cautioned to keep a look-out for other
of the game, which was probably in other ravines, and
would run for the prairie as soon as they 'winded' the
hunters.

"As the mounted men reached the upland, probably two
thousand buffalo, in small herds, were in sight, some of
them not more than two hundred yards away.   The
charge was ordered, and, 'every man for himself,' the
hunters started.   I kept up the chase till both my revol-
vers were emptied, and had dropped three, and then
pulled up to find myself alone, and more than a mile from
the nearest hunter.

"There was always one danger in running buffalo in the
Indian Country.   The hunter, engrossed solely in the pursuit of his game, lost all idea of course or distance, and a
run of four or five miles was not an unusual thing, and
at the end of that the sportsman found himself alone on
the prairie, with empty pistols and a tired-out steed, in a
most defenceless state if suddenly attacked.

"I was soon joined by the other officer, and we waited for the wagon to come up and get our game, in the mean time scanning the ground along the horizon for some sign of the ambulance. But we looked in vain, and as soon as the beef was loaded we retraced our steps in search of the Professor. Nearly two miles back we met one of the party, his face wearing a disgusted look, as though *he* did not think much of buffalo-hunting. To our inquiries about the others he replied,—

"'I don't know where they are. The driver took us up to that place you pointed out, and just as we reached it a small herd came rushing up from the ravines, and "the old man" told us to get out and get a shot, and as we jumped out another herd came along, and he told the driver to drive on, and left us out in the cold, and by that time the herd we had first seen had run off out of reach. The last I saw of the team it was away off in that direction (pointing to the southwest), and I think it was running away.'

"Turning in the direction indicated, we galloped off in search of the lost man, and rode nearly two miles before, as much farther away, we saw the ambulance halted, and a man apparently at work on a carcass. Riding up, we found the team all right, and the Professor at work. He *was* a sight! Had killed a young bull (as the driver told it, 'had filled him too full of lead for him to carry'), had lost his hat, and in lieu of it had tied a white hand-kerchief about his head,—thrown off his coat, and, with only a knife 'hacked worse than two saws,' and which had been used all the trip for digging fossils, he was en-deavoring to cut off the animal's head as a trophy. His hands and arms were bloody, his face dripped with per-spiration, and in trying to wipe it away he had forgotten that his hands were bloody, and had stained face, hair and the handkerchief with gore, till he looked worse than a Chicago butcher. We sent the driver back to bring up the wagon, and then proceeded to assist in getting off the skin, as he said he must have it dressed and the head mounted. After he had returned to the post, had a bath, and cooled down mentally, he began to think how he must have looked and acted, and after his return to the East it was soon a tabooed subject. The driver's story, told to his fellows, was expressed in language more forcible than eloquent. Leaving out the expletives, it was about as follows :

" '*He* wasn't goin' to shoot no buffalo ! Oh, no ! But after he got them young fellows out, he jest went plumb crazy, an' when about the third bunch of 'em run past, he poked his gun out past my head an' fired right over my mules, an' they *went* in spite o' me. His hat blowed off, and I wanted to go back fur it, but he sung out not to mind the hat, but go on, and bime by he banged away again, and then the buffaler stopped, an' I began to circle 'round him, and then the old fellow jumped out and was goin' to run right up on him ; till I hollowed that he'd git histed if he did, and then he jest stood off, and pumped lead into him till he dropped. Talk about " buck ager "—if he didn't have " buffaler fever " I'm a tenderfoot.'

" The Professor came back the next year, and with him came one of the same party. Scarcely had we shaken hands when he said, ' Don't say buffalo to the old gentleman,—it is a sore subject.' "

" And now it is time we had a love story," exclaimed Mrs. Grace. " And there's one man at least whom I know will do the subject justice. Most of you have no idea of it. Come, Major," and she glanced at a tall, soldierly fellow sitting about midway along the joyous line to her left. All eyes are already centred on him. In love or war "the Major" was regarded as thoroughly at home.

"Drive on, Major. If any one has been there, it's you," exclaimed Briggs from his seat across the board.

No direct reply was vouchsafed the light-hearted young gentleman. With much dignity of mien the Major waited until the applause which greeted this especial call had subsided, bowed to the lady of the bright blue eyes and then to the table collectively, and began.

TOM CARRINGTON'S CHRISTMAS GIFT.

"Lieutenant Tom Carrington accounted himself an invulnerable man so far as matters affecting the heart were concerned. He had gone through 'West Point' a shining light in the 'Bachelors' Club,' the only known departure from the tenets of his faith having been an enforced five minutes' chat with Miss Mabel Stoughton, as he stood in his official capacity, watch in hand, at the door of the hop-room, waiting to give that awful signal which put an abrupt termination to tête-à-têtes, and stilled the glowing words upon beardless lips. This interview, short and unsought as it was, brought upon him some measure of suspicion, but he heroically lived it down and went out into the world the following June, with an escutcheon undimmed by any act of abrogation of his oath. But five minutes' conversation with Miss Mabel Stoughton was apt to create strange havoc even in the strong-hold of youthful susceptibility, and as Tom Carrington walked to camp that night he was forced to acknowledge to himself a remarkably pleasant sensation, and he seemed to hear a faint melody as of silver bells, which he coupled with Mabel's voice and before his eyes was the remem-

bered glint upon 'curls of summer gold,' enframing a fair
young face.   But he shook himself together and devoted
the rest of the night to the 'plebs' who were on guard,
who, could they have known the cause of his extra attention to duty, would in their hearts have heartily cursed
that five minutes' delay in the beating of the drum.

"In the winter of 188– the Judith Basin was sparsely
settled—only here and there, and that at long intervals,
low, rambling sheep-sheds proclaimed the nearness of a
Ranch.   Time-honored signs had given the ranchmen
ample indications of the coming of a rigorous winter, and
fabulous wood-piles and tons of well-stacked hay stood as
answer to the warning. Beyond the mountains, mostly
amid the foot-hills, a few hastily constructed huts served
as shelter to a little colony of soldiers, dropped there as
a nucleus of an army post. Herds of buffalo ranged over
the rolling prairie-land towards the west, and among the
foot-hills elk and deer and antelope, grouse and prairie-
hen were as yet innocent of the invasion of their realm.
Centrally through the valley a rushing, bubbling trout
stream tumbled its limpid waters toward the Mussel-shell,
musical in its flow, freighted with the traditions of the hills.
And these stately hills, stretching north and south in rugged, wild upheaval, hiding the crimson and passionate hues
outlining the purple shadows of the west from the gentler
suggestions of the nascent day, like kingly sentinels in crest
and nodding plume, dominated the far reaches of nature's
gentler aspect, toward the rising and the setting sun. Busily
the little colony worked from dawn to dark upon the rude
shelters which were their only hope against the ruder
blasts and snows of coming winter ; already the voices of
the pines upon the mountain were hoarse and muttering,
and here and there a peak, higher than its neighbors, had
caught the hoary mask of Time and proclaimed the

already numbered days of the fading year. Bedecked in sombre vestment, the darkening mountain lay waiting for the shock of winter's battle, with here and there a crimson gleam of ivy showing, like a 'rose which the west has flung' within the coil of a woman's raven hair while along its rugged sides the echoes played of hammer and axe and human call from the busy slope below. But time and labor accomplish most things and November's sway had scarce begun when the little garrison was snug as need be for the winter. Only a couple of companies constituted the garrison, with a Major in command, and two short of the half-dozen officers whose names were borne upon the rolls; but, then, there was the Dr., and he was worth the other two and one to spare, beside.

"There had been a good deal of speculation among the juniors as to why the Major insisted upon that extra room with two windows, with a southern exposure, especially as time was limited and the men overworked beside, and when, upon mutual inspection and comparison of the preparation for the long months to come, the dainty fitting of this apartment was revealed to their astonished gaze, with its light oak furnishing and accessory of blue and white, its heavy rugs and bright warm curtains ready to swing into graceful folds in opposition to encroaching blasts, 'Confusion was worse confounded,' and Mrs. Wilder vouchsafed no explanation and the Major held his peace as a wise and dutiful husband should.

"A couple of evenings later, Dr. Archer and Lieutenant Bliss, of the —th foot, were seated within the rather narrow limits of that particular log hut which had been reared for the accommodation of themselves and one other, and which had been considered in the present emergency adequate to the dignity of their rank and years, and were in the enjoyment of one of those pauses in their game of

chess which the replenishment of the fire and their pipes
required, and had, for the moment, forgotten the very
threatening attitude which the Dr.'s Queen's Bishop had,
by a masterly play just assumed, to discuss the important
matter as to whether lemon was an adjunct or real necessity in a ' hot scotch ' brew—when Lieutenant Tom Carrington and a gust of wind darted simultaneously into
the room to the extinguishment of the light and the temporary change of subject. ' Why the devil don't you
come down the chimney, Tom, or give notice of your
approach—one might prepare against the combination of
Tom Carrington and Boreas in such a case.'

" ' Teddy, I'm truly sorry, for light has such a mellowing
influence upon your voice and,' scratching a match, ' I'll
wager anything that you fellows are in your hearts glad to
be rid of the sight of each other even for a moment ; but,
there you are again, so take up the thread of your argu-
ment, and peace be unto you,' and Mr. Carrington began
softly whistling an air from Erminie, as he divested himself of top-coat and boots, and encased his feet in his slippers and his form in his smoking jacket. ' By the way,
did anybody say—Welcome ! Tom ? for if not, there may
be a dearth of information, which I am prepared to
impart.'

" ' Welcome ! Tom—thrice welcome ! ' came in chorus
from two pairs of healthy lungs. What is it ? Hurry up,
delays are dangerous—suspense, death.'

" ' Gently, gentlemen ; gentle subjects should be approached with deference, and, indeed, upon second
thought, I think it hardly decorous to utter a young
lady's name in an atmosphere reeking with tobacco and
lemon and things, as this is. I won't ; but shall simply
content myself with the announcement that unto the
house of Mrs. Major Wilder a guest is coming for the

winter, and that guest is a young lady, and that now the
mystery of the "spare-room" is settled and that to-morrow I, Thomas Carrington of the —th foot, depart upon a
journey, "and further deponent saith not,"' and the
notes of the lullaby song in Erminie fell upon the air
once more, and a wreath of smoke from the lips of Lieutenant Carrington went curling toward the mantel, in an
interval of pause.

"'And is that all that we are to hear ; will your Lordship
deign not one other word upon this momentous matter,'
exclaimed Teddy Bliss with a tone of genuine exaspera-
tion.

"'The subject is dismissed, gentlemen ; you may resume
your game,' remarked Carrington with the mock tones of a
commanding officer ; and the others knew, with all his
assumed mannerism, that he had his own reasons for saying no more upon the subject ; but Teddy Bliss could not
resist the temptation of a final word which assumed the
rather indefinite form of—' Well, I'll be ——'

"'Indeed you will, Teddy,' interrupted Carrington, 'if
you do not control that unruly member,' and with the
expression of the hope that his companions might have
sweet repose, happy dreams, sweet tempers and patience,
he filed into the little alcove which he designated his
'sleeping apartment' and disappeared for the night.

"By way of preparation, not only for the expected visitor, but also for the long months of isolation staring the
little garrison in the face, Major Wilder had despatched
an 'escort wagon' to the nearest town (some hundred
miles distant) for such articles of comfort and luxury as
the Inspector General had not recommended as necessary
or advisable among the 'stores which may be sold for
cash' to officers of the U. S. Army, and this wagon was
to call on its return at a certain ranch in the Judith Basin

3*

for such luggage as Miss Mabel Stoughton might see fit
to turn over to its driver, which latter part of the programme had remained a matter 'lacking announcement'
until a few moments before Lieutenant Carrington's
abrupt entrance into the society of the Doctor and Lieutenant Bliss, and the subsequent interchange of the
amenities of social converse cited above.

" On this particular evening, with some degree of mental speculation as to the nature of Mrs. Wilder's 'matter
of importance' concerning which she wished to see Lieutenant Carrington, that young gentleman had hastened
to her quarters, and had received so much of the information regarding the matter at issue as has been already
imparted to the reader—and more. Partially in fulfillment, Mrs. Wilder explained, of a long-standing engagement with her Boston friend and schoolmate, Miss
Edith Barnes, whose father was trying the experiment of
a 'Sheep Ranch' in the Judith Basin, in the hope of
regaining some of the health which the east-wind of
Boston had seriously impaired, and partly that she might
be within hailing distance, as it were, of his half-sister,
Mrs. Wilder, when that lady should be ready to receive
her, Miss Stoughton had been only a day's ride from them
for several weeks, and the appointed time of her visit to
the post had arrived. The Major had intended riding
over for her himself, but he was suffering so much with
his old enemy, the gout, that he found it impossible to go
and, would not Lieutenant Carrington come to the rescue?
She knew she could trust Mabel to him, knowing that
he would take the best of care of her. He could go over
on the following day and return the next, staying the
intervening night at the ranch. Of Miss Mabel Stoughton's relationship to Mrs. Major Wilder the young man
had been profoundly ignorant till that very moment. In

the one year and a half he had been away from the
'academy,' his mind had often reverted to that five minutes at the hop-room door, and always with a certain
thrill of pleasure which he could not understand. He
had never, that he remembered, met any one quite so fair
as she had seemed to him during the shortness of his
interview—'the rose lip's witching glow' upon the cheek,
her golden hair, the tone of her low and musical voice,
he had often thought of them ; but he had never thought
to meet her again.   There had been no 'bliss at meeting,
no parting pain.'   She had been but a fair figure upon
the fair earth, as it passed by his point of view, so that
Mrs. Wilder's request somewhat staggered him.

" ' I am always at your service, Mrs. Wilder,' he replied, 'and shall be most happy, if you think the young
lady will not fear to venture—what did you say was
the name?' and as he heard it repeated he looked as
though it had never dwelt pleasantly upon his ear before,
and felt as though that kind destiny, which shapes our
ends, overshadowed him.

" As Carrington approached the ranch the following
afternoon the tones of a piano smote upon his ear in ac-
companiment to two voices, which came to him

> 'Like the sweet South
> That breathes upon a bank of violets ;'

so he paused and listened till the music ceased, and, looking far off toward the distant hills, over the stretches of
lonely prairie, into the unfathomable depths of trackless
grass-land innocent of human habitation, thought how
little it took to give the semblance of beauty to the world's
waste places.   But if his surprise were great, it was not
more so than that of the two young ladies who, hearing the
sound of wheels, turned to look upon the tall, handsome

young officer who was reining in at the door and who a moment later presented his credentials in form of a letter from Mrs. Wilder. There was no instant recognition on Miss Mabel's part of her former unwilling captive. His appearance seemed to feebly awaken some memory, but nothing very tangible; not till the drift of conversation led back to the 'Point' and individual experience there, did it dawn upon her that in her coming escort she beheld the 'member in good standing' of the 'Bachelor Club.'

"'It was very good of you, Mr. Carrington, to so far subdue your principles as to consent to an eight-hour drive with a young lady to whom you once begrudged five minutes,' remarked Miss Mabel as that evening they were speaking of the morrow's ride.

"'I think my principles only awaked, where your sex is concerned, after graduation, Miss Stoughton. I hadn't quite formed any before; I was rather afraid of the subject, you see,' replied Carrington. 'Really, though, I hope to atone for any past sins of omission by religious devotion to your sex in the future. Pray accept yourself my first cry of surrender.'

"'It will be hard upon you, I know, but I will promise to be very generous and help you through the ordeal,' said Mabel; 'but tell me, Mr. Carrington, did you ever forgive me for entrapping you that night?'

"'I think the drum was all that saved me from absolute capitulation—there is a note of forgiveness in that confession, is there not?' answered Carrington.

"As they were talking, the rumble of wheels heralded the approach of the wagon, and as the start was to be an early one, the young lady's trunks were loaded that night, and the next morning, before the sun had climbed one-third the way to the zenith, Carrington and his fair charge were bowling along toward the Judith River.

" It was Sunday morning and there was a Sabbath tone in the air, and Carrington stole a glance at the lovely girl beside him ; he did not wonder that it 'seemed no task for the sun to shine upon so fair a picture.' Altogether the young gentleman's state was a happy one, and he mentally evoked a blessing upon the Major for his opportune attack of gout, upon Mrs. Wilder, first, for having so sweet a sister, and again for her part in his assignment to the pleasant duty before him—blessed that strange fate, in fine, which had laid his lines in such pleasant places. But a single little cloud drifted across the sky of his content, which assumed the features of that arch-tormentor, Mr. Teddy Bliss. He could hear in anticipation that young man's congratulations upon his success in having achieved a triumph over his well-known diffidence ; he could hear the pointed shafts which should inquire as to the probable duration of his willingness to associate with ordinary humanity, and whether he (Teddy) would be expected to indulge a new suit in view of the coming event ; he knew he would stop at nothing, and he was very fond of Teddy, but—'well, if he does I shall simply choke him, and that's all about it,' was his mental resolve.

" 'What did you say, Mr. Carrington ?' inquired Miss Mabel, rather astonished at the unexpectedness of this last part of Tom's unwittingly-outspoken resolve ; ' whom do you wish to choke ; not me, I trust !'

" 'I beg pardon,' pleaded Carrington ; ' I was thinking of——'

" 'Never mind his name,' interrupted Mabel, 'but please retain your faculties in this immediate vicinity ; that off-horse of yours will need all the attention which I can afford to dispense with myself.'

" 'Oh, he's all right ; he has only caught the infection

of happiness from his master; besides, he is proud of his burden to-day.'

"And at that moment a 'coyote' slunk across the road, and his horse, not liking the skulking brute's appearance, made a dash for freedom, and for a couple of hundred yards Carrington had his hands full; but he presently quieted them down, and, looking at Mabel, who had behaved admirably, remarked : 'Splendid, Miss Stoughton; you're a trump !'

"'Thank you,' said Mabel, who was pale as death, but could not resist the interrogatory : 'Of what suit, Mr. Carrington ? '

"'Hearts, of course ; but here's the river ;' and Carrington noticed that under the influence of the 'Chinook,' which had come up in the night, it had risen, and he concluded to see the wagon over safely before crossing himself.

"Looking at his watch, he found it just high noon, and a few moments later the wagon came rumbling down the hill behind them, and, at a sign from him, dashed into the stream, struck boldly across, and, when nearly at the other bank, stalled. There was a led horse behind the wagon, and he, taking advantage of the situation, proceeded to drink ; but scarcely had his lips touched the water when there came from up the river a sound as of a dozen cannons, and a moment later huge blocks of ice, impelled with terrific speed, bore down upon the stalled wagon. Faster and faster came the ice ; higher and higher it piled against the wagon's side, which now listed down stream. A moment more and animals and vehicle would be swept away in the irresistible flow. 'Cut the traces and save the animals and yourself,' shouted Carrington, which, with the assistance of a man to whom he had given a 'lift,' the driver was able to do, and an instant later down the seething, on-rushing, pitiless flood, wagon and led-horse—first one on top, then the other—disappeared round a curve, five hundred feet below. Carrington's first thought was of Mabel's trunks, and they found expression :

"'My God! Miss Stoughton, your trunks, your trunks!'

"'I was thinking of that poor horse,' she said ; 'if only you can save him ! His look of dumb despair will haunt me forever.'

"'That's the gentlewoman of it,' said Carrington. 'Wait here till I run down the bank, the wagon may have lodged,' and true enough, hurled by the force of the water in a head of the stream, it had been thrown upon a sand-bar high and dry, or nearly so, and in the midst, with a look of patient inquiry upon his face, stood the led-horse, intact. To cross themselves was impossible, and their wagon was ruined, the hind wheels gone and it a wreck.

Mr. Carrington's trying situation had hitherto been the result of a sympathetic relationship with the heroes of those sensational works which had chanced to come to his notice ; the last few moments had assigned to himself the principal part in what seemed to him a most tragic one. Retreat was impossible, for behind him every 'coulee' by this time was a torrent itself ; he felt himself impelled to quick and decisive action.

"'Miss Stoughton,' he said ; 'our position is one of the most extreme embarrassment ; we can neither go back or forward. I shall send one of these men to the Post for succor. Will you give yourself into my keeping, freely, as my own sister would, feeling that I will care for you as tenderly. Your bed must be upon the prairie, but with the wraps and robe in the buggy I can at least shelter you from cold.'

"Mabel Stoughton had as stout a heart as ever beat within a woman's breast, but certainly it was put now to a crucial test. She had lost everything and now found herself, at the approach of night, alone upon the broad prairie with a man whom she had known for five minutes only, before he had come, the night previous, to take her for an eight hours' ride through an almost uninhabited country, but that man wore the cloth which proclaimed to her the gentleman in every man who donned it and she never faltered. She saw Carrington's distress and pitied him. Putting her little hand in his, she looked up to him with eyes all full of pity and of trust, and simply said : 'Fate has overtaken us, my friend ; we will brave it out together.'

" 'God bless you !' he answered ; 'you have given me the fairest glimpse of womanhood I have ever known.'

" It was long after midnight—the moon had been looking calmly down, shedding a dower of light upon the earth and silvering the surface of the rushing water. Scarcely a breath of air was stirring, but it was growing colder. High up above the tree-tops, over in the west, a few clouds came drifting lazily along—occasionally a moan came from the distant hillside—the bark of a dog, distant, indistinct, from somewhere beyond the river, fell upon the watcher's ears, sharp, insistent—an owl's unfriendly hoot sounded in hollow mockery—the shadows which the moon had painted lengthened out into the plain, shifting slowly and in grotesque shapes—the weird impressions of the night filled all of Nature's spaces. Carrington was looking with some dread at the drifting clouds, knowing that in every one of them was 'some story of storm to come or past,' and he prayed that God would temper the wind to his precious charge. Just then a coyote barked and Mabel awoke.

" 'Were you praying, Mr. Carrington?' she asked.

" 'Execrating that coyote for having disturbed you Miss Stoughton.'

" 'No, sir! you were praying, and I waked up to say Amen! good-night,' she said.

> " 'And the stillness was unbroken
> And the silence gave no token,'

till by and by a faint flush crept over the eastern hills and brought across the 'threshold of the skies' the blessedness of dawn.

" An inspection of the river discovered the feasibility of crossing; the waters which the day before had burst through the the ice-dam, carrying ruin in their path, had passed by, leaving a wreck to tell the story of their fury —now the stream flowed musically on and nothing barred the way to progress. The ominous clouds which had so disturbed Carrington during the night had dissolved, the canopy of heaven was one unbroken field of blue and, as the pink of dawn brightened into the golden glory of day, the travelers left the river behind them and headed for the distant hills. Midway between the scene of their mishap and the post they met the relief party, which they sent to gather up what they could from the wreck and, a couple of hours later, Carrington deposited his charge at the door of the Major's hut and in the arms of her anxious sister. Leaving her, Carrington said, 'You will understand, if I do not call this evening?' and for a moment Mabel did not understand, but an instant later she appreciated his thoughtful kindness and thanked him in her heart.

" Of course, speculation as to the non-appearance of the travelers was rife throughout the little settlement the night before; the Major's gout, owing to his excited state of mind, gave him an added twinge, which in no way tended to temper his irascibility. Mrs. Wilder, kind and gentle woman that she was, felt that some good reason had detained them ; but Mrs. McFarlane, whose forty-five years of 'following the drum' had been innocent of any known expression of charitable thought for any human being, shook her head ominously, till the little curls at the back of her neck danced like puppets upon the expanding field of her fair shoulders. To her Lieut. Teddy Bliss felt himself constrained, in defence of his friend, to remark that he had known Miss Stoughton for some time, and Lieut. Carrington for years—that both belonged to that category of gentility to whom a compromising situation was impossible, and that he regretted the enforced conviction that there were some people, who did not, with which satisfying shot he left the object of his remarks to pursue undisturbed her communing with the stars, and passed on and into the seclusion of his own domain. Mabel, as was to be expected, took the garrison by storm ; her beauty, the gracious and gentle manner which she had for all, from the Major down to the striker, won her only friends, and under the modifying influences which she exerted, even Teddy Bliss dropped his cynicism and became a wonder of metamorphosis.

" The last month of the year had come and the storm kings were gathering their forces ; the little garrison gave over its excursions to distant points, in deference to the ominous mutterings of winter. Cards and cosy little suppers, rambles over the neighboring hills, and occasional forays upon the Ranch, down the valley, filled up the spaces of their time. Carrington had no occasion to 'choke' Teddy Bliss ; that young gentleman's views of life underwent perceptible modification, and few were the days when, at one hour or another, he did not saunter over to the Major's 'for the bracer the sight of that splendid girl gives one, you know,' as he said to the Doctor. Carrington's position toward the young lady he defined more accurately himself than others who had busied themselves in the matter. He had become very fond of Mabel, of course, as had everybody, but he had said no word of love to her ; he did not flatter himself that she would be inclined to listen if he did ; the accident that had thrown them together, under circumstances out of common, had no bearing, to his mind, upon the case at all—in fact, it would have rather had the effect of retarding any declaration, had he thought of making one. Once or twice, of a night, when he and Teddy and the Doctor were sitting round the blazing logs, within the enclosure of their own four walls, and, tired of talk, had settled themselves, with their pipes, for a little self-communing, before bidding each other and the world goodnight, his fancy had wrought out of the glowing coals pictures fair to look upon, and from out the picture looking up at him were eyes of heaven's own blue, and within his own, a little hand, soft and warm, lay passively, with now and then a gentle pressure responsive to a heart-beat, and as the ashes settled white and thick upon the embers, and the fading light had its suggestion of clouds drifting across his sky (the shadows of earthly trouble), the pressure of the hand grew stronger, and from out the gloom a soft, sweet voice seemed to come laden with the tones of comfort and the accents of hope, and, yielding to the soothing influences of the hour, and of his fancy, he would close his eyes and let this 'dream of delicate beauty melt into his heart's recess.'

" The Christmas season was fast approaching, and ever-greens and rose-berries and such pretty grasses as reared their nodding tassels above the snow were brought into requisition wherewith to bedeck their humble dwellings, and on Christmas eve there had been a supper party and some singing at the Major's, and Teddy had announced that he proposed to hang up his stocking and thought, considering his youth, that Carrington should do the same, and the ladies had all agreed that if they did they should find them filled in the morning, and Carrington had asked ' Mabel ' what he might expect from her, and she had told him that really she did not know ; that, after Mr. Bliss' remark, she should have to think of something suited to his years, at which Mrs. Wilder spoke up and said : ' Don't worry, Mr. Carrington ; I might tell you more about that myself than I shall ; wait and see.'   And as the little clock upon the mantel chimed out the midnight hour a very fair chorus of voices sang a Christmas hymn and so they parted.   For several days a large body of Indians had been camped some three or four miles below the park, a few of whom had been in to exchange a friendly greeting, and a night or two previous two or three of them, having obtained some liquor, became troublesome and, indeed, had fired upon the guard in their effort to expel them, but nobody had been hurt and the Major had let it go, thinking it only a drunken, crazy freak which would not be repeated.   Christmas Day dawned bright and beautiful, and many of the men had early set off to hunt in the mountains, leaving but a very small number to guard the Post.   There had been some talk of a sleigh-ride in the afternoon down to the Ranch, but an incident occurred which changed the plans of all concerned and brought the speculations of Mrs. O'Keefe and some others to an end.

"Toward the middle of the morning there appeared down the valley, far as the eye could reach, a long,

black moving line winding in and out through the curv-
ings of the road and becoming gradually more distinct.
Carrington was standing with Mabel near the Major's
door admiring the wintry picture outspread before them,
and she had just told him that for his audacity the night
before in asking for it, she should not give him the present she had intended, and he had begged to be placed on
probation till the New Year, when their eyes chanced to
rest upon this long, dark, moving mass, filing into the
plain below them and form into line, then move slowly
forward.   There were some two hundred warriors, splen-
didly mounted—equipped for battle—the sunlight flashing from their rifle-barrels, their gaudy feathers tossing
in the wind.   Steadily they moved forward, chanting a
wild, weird song, while before them one warrior rode from
right to left and left to right in wild careering, flourishing
a scalp-lock upon a pole and evidently leading in the song.
One by one they saw the men slip quickly within their
quarters and then reappear.   It was a new sight to Carrington.   It might mean nothing—it might mean much.
To Mabel it meant everything.   But the one idea had
fastened upon her brain.   It was to be but the repetition
of Fetterman and the Little Big Horn, and as Carrington
turned to go, saying he would find out what it was and
come soon to tell her, and noticed the look of terror upon
her face, he knew that her fears were not for herself alone.
Looking again at the line he saw it halted, and the leader
in parley with the officer of the day.

"'See, Mabel,' he said ; 'it is nothing—only a Christmas visit ; but may not I have this for my Christmas gift ?'
And he stooped and kissed her, and Mrs. Wilder from
her point of vantage at the window saw, and mutely sent
them her blessing."

"It's the Quartermaster's turn," suggested Miss Dot

at this moment, while people were glancing about the table as though in search of the next victim.

"Yes, of course," loudly seconded Mr. Briggs. "Come, Vouchers, something's got to be done to redeem the Staff since X.'s fizzle."

The Colonel laughed as he turned to his junior staff officer. "Never you mind what Briggs says, Mr. Quartermaster. The staff can take care of itself."

"That's precisely the trouble, Colonel," shouted the irrepressible Briggs. "What we would like is that the staff should occasionally take care of somebody else." Whereat there was a burst of laughter. The line is ever ready to applaud a hit at the staff. But the Quartermaster only grinned—and began :

THE QUARTERMASTER'S STORY.

"Shortly before the 55th Cavalry was ordered to Arizona, Captain Sabres had quite an acquisition to his troop in the person of his second lieutenant ; and as he occupies a somewhat prominent position in this narrative, a brief description seems almost unavoidable.

"Imagine 'Granville de Vigne,' 'Sabretasche,' 'Curly,' or any other *beau sabreur* who is 'Ouida's' conception of a cavalryman ; then divest him of his paraphernalia and habiliments, place to his credit the moderate bank account of the average second lieutenant, allow him quarters and emoluments in accordance with his rank, and you will have a fair idea of Lieutenant Evan Tavistock.

"He was of that same immaculate order of being as those sybarites whom I cite, and fancied his environment in every way similar to theirs. One meeting him and conversing on such topics as his antique bronzes, his old master paintings, his rare china, his thoroughbreds and his traps, would scarcely believe that his sleeping apartment was carpetless and his ivory bedstead a common hospital cot. But such was really the case; and his exaggerated style and absurd pretention soon made him the laughing stock of the regiment.

"Nevertheless he was so thoroughly good-hearted and unselfish, bore chaffing so well, and was all in all such a divine, undisguised ass that none could truthfully say they disliked him.

"Mr. Tavistock had been in Arizona about one month when he was ordered out in pursuit of deserters. He reached Fort Burns—forty miles distant—and there tarried; sending the sergeant on after the fugitives, because it was such a 'blawsted bore' to go himself. When he learned that there were three brides and several young women at Burns, he felt greatly annoyed that he had not fetched a few of his trunks. To be sure he had his top-boots with their silver screw spurs, and his visorless cap upon his person; but his wardrobe consisted of his corduroy breeches and a jacket with huge orange plush shoulder-straps. He felt in a measure relieved when he perceived that his attire was entirely unlike that of the other officers; it implied distinction, he thought. At the same time he could not fancy it the correct thing in connection with brides, young women and dinner parties. He liked the garrison immensely; and there he enjoyed himself during the week that his sergeant was taking in Tucson's places of amusement in quest of the missing troopers.

"Though it did not take the veterans at Burns long to diagnose Mr. Tavistock's case, yet by the ladies he was pronounced perfectly charming. In describing to them his surroundings at Fort Davenport, he had used 'de

Vigne's own words; and it was not easy for these credulous ones to believe it was all fancy or deception. In taking leave of them, he invited all to eat their Christmas dinner with him at Davenport, promising them wild turkeys and other good things. He even went so far as to tell the belle of the garrison that if she would agree to come, he would run over for her and 'tool her down in his tilbury!'

"Not long after his return to Davenport Lieutenant De Canter had occasion to visit Burns on official business. While there he naturally heard much of Tavistock, and learned many details respecting the young man's visit. He was not surprised to hear of the glowing account Tavistock had given of Davenport—of his quarters, his horses and his traps—for that was the creature's way. But he really was amazed when he learned of the general invitation to dine with him, which several of the fair ones were anxious to accept. One of them, in fact, came to De Canter and begged him to use his influence with Mrs. Trolls to persuade her to chaperon them.

"De Canter reflected that it might be a capital scheme to let the ladies go over, anticipating a royal dinner with Tavistock, he not to know of their advent until too late to provide for them. This would naturally mortify him, and might result in curing him of his absurd conceit. De Canter had little difficulty in persuading Mrs. Trolls to go, and he advised the beauty not to wait for Mr. Tavistock and his 'tilbury,' but to come in the regulation army landau, with its mule motive-power.

"De Canter chuckled to himself as he mused on his diplomacy, and the huge joke he had put up on Tavistock. But it might have been more huge, had it not been of that common brand—'too good to keep.' He felt that he must have some one to enjoy it with him; so before he had been back at Davenport half an hour he had let two others into the secret. These regarded it precisely as he had, so they followed his example and told others; consequently the whole garrison, Tavistock included, knew of the entire plan a whole week before Christmas.

"When it was learned that Tavistock was well informed on the subject, general regret was expressed. De Canter tried to defend his loquacity by saying it would be an utter impossibility for the fellow to give a decent dinner any way; and, as the invited guests were surely coming, the awkwardness of Tavistock's position would be just as great.

"From this date poor Tavistock was made the target for no end of chaff. The fellows went for him unmercifully, asking him if the dinner was to be 'a la Russe' or 'How?' If the turkey was to be stuffed with his old puns in lieu of chestnuts, and if he expected to catch his *menu* card in the draw. These and similar asininities, well calculated to annoy and exasperate, had no effect whatsoever upon Tavistock. In fact he accepted all their chaff pleasantly, and in the most approved Hyde Park fashion.

"There were others in the garrison, however, who were far more exercised as day after day passed and they saw no preparation being made for the promised repast; and they wondered how Tavistock expected to escape from his dilemma. He apparently never gave the matter a thought, but was far from idle. When he finally comprehended that there was on foot a preconcerted scheme to embarrass and make him appear ridiculous, he at once determined to do the best he could in the way of a dinner. And with this resolve buried in his heart and sealed on his lips, he sought the post trader. From this individual he, for a modest stipend, borrowed everything he could

4

possibly need in the way of china, glasses, knives, forks
and spoons.   His own trunks furnished the table linen,
which was of fine quality, having once graced the table
of his great-grandfather.   With the assistance of his
striker, he had already purloined from vacant quarters
several tables—the property of the government—and
these, when arranged in line and covered with a handsome cloth, really made a very respectable banquet board.
Horseshoe-nails were substituted for nut-picks, just because they smacked of the service ; and having quietly
and satisfactorily attended to these preliminaries, he de-
tailed a man from his troop to act as *chef*, and ordered the
great dinner.

"It was the 25th of December.   Tavistock regarded it
as a stroke of good fortune that he was officer-of-the-day.
The guests, who would shortly arrive, were sufficiently
conversant with army matters to know that many duties
pertained to this office, and would excuse his frequent ab-
sences.   Time would thus be given him, to be used to his
own advantage.   'Besides,' he reflected ; 'I only asked
them to dine ; not to put up with me.'

"In due time two ambulances from Fort Burns bowled
into the garrison.   Mrs. Trolls, Mrs. Hinton and four
young ladies had accepted the kind invitation of Mr.
Tavistock ; so had—unasked—Captain Trolls and Mr.
Newburg.   But these, as well as the entire party, were
assured by the officer-of-the-day that he was 'chawmed
no end' to see them.   Then they were spirited away by
different inmates of the garrison, better situated to dispose of them, temporarily, than the would-be swell host.

"Tavistock had announced the dinner-hour as six
o'clock ; and as the appointed time drew near, much speculation was indulged in, especially by the inmates of the
garrison, respecting Tavistock's plans.   The fact that he

had really provided anything never, for one moment, entered their minds.

"At the proper time the company assembled at Mr. Tavistock's quarters, where he warmly received them. He was arrayed as immaculately as permissible with the office he had that day filled His quarters had been tidied up a little by McGoon, his striker; that was all. There was an absence of bric-a-brac, *bijouterie*, and in fact of all ornamentation and decoration, which must have struck the visitors as peculiar, when recalling the previous description they had received. But naturally, only such remarks as: 'Why, how nicely you are fixed!' 'How pleasantly you are situated!' and other similar flatteries were indulged in.

"Some little time ensued, and the garrison guests present were showing symptoms of impatience, when a neighboring door was thrust open and McGoon, in swallow-tail coat and white apron, in stentorian tones shouted: 'Cum a runnin' !'

"It must be admitted that the words fell like a blow on the ear of the elegant and refined host; but the mirth occasioned by the plebeian announcement soon banished all embarrassment, and, giving his arm to Mrs. Trolls, he passed into the adjoining room, followed by the rest of the company.

"Great, indeed, was the surprise of every one. There stretched a long table, neatly covered with spotless linen, whose purity and fineness was at once remarked upon. The silver knives and forks shone brightly beneath the many lights, and there was nothing to indicate that they were borrowed or plated. The china was a trifle superior —as were also the glasses—to the average Arizona table-furniture; and the centre-piece, towering from its mesquite embankment, was abundantly and tastefully filled with fruit from the commissary. The whole scene was really quite attractive and alluring.

"After a brief survey of his surroundings, Lieutenant De Canter, who was one of the guests, so far recovered from his amazement as to mentally articulate: 'I'll be d—— !' But hope had not quite deserted him; he remembered the promised turkey, and well knowing that one had never been seen in or around Davenport, felt, in a measure, assured. Others of the garrison present were also greatly astonished; but the visitors accepted it all as a matter of course.

"McGoon and Flynn—a brother trooper, who was acting assistant—brought in the soup, which was pronounced faultless. Then Flynn approached the host and asked: 'Will the loot'unt have the lemmin edd now?'

"'Er—ah, yes; you howling idiot;' muttered poor Tavistock; and a moment later, while the company were convulsed with laughter, the well-disguised troopers were filling the glasses with 'lemmin edd,' flowing from bottles whose labels were a guarantee of the excellence of their contents.

"All were cheerful; everything was passing off delightfully, and—yes, here comes McGoon with the promised turkey, which he deftly places before the composed host.

"'Oh, how lovely!' 'How awfully nice in you!' and other similar expressions from the visitors greeted Tavistock, as he recklessly replied:

"'Told you I'd knock you one over, you know; they're as thick as cweam awound here.'

"Then came the vegetables—canned to be sure; but who would suspect it, when prepared by a troop *chef* and served in McGoon's *recherché* style.

"And here comes the 'rum-pudding,' as Flynn called it, 'blazing fer al the woorled loike a bloomin' shell!'

"So far Tavistock had no reason to feel ashamed of his spread. It is doubtful if another in the garrison could have done better. Many and sincere were the congratulations he received, and one fair guest remarked to him she wished the officers at Burns were half so nice and thoughtful.

"In addition to the astonishment which De Canter experienced, he felt decidedly cheap; his supreme joke had proved no joke at all. He did not enjoy his dinner because his skin did not fit him, as he afterwards expressed it. He felt ill at ease, and, fancying a soupçon of cognac might benefit him, strolled back to the dining-room to help himself; but McGoon—and McGoon in tears—anticipated his wish.

"'Why, what's the matter, McGoon?' he asked, as he tossed off the brandy. 'Has anything gone wrong with you?'

"'There's not a dhry oieye in the throope, loot'unt;' sobbed the old soldier.

"'What do you mean?' asked the thoroughly perplexed subaltern.

"'The pet's kilt! murdurhed!' was the reply.

"'What pet are you talking about?' inquired De Canter.

"'"F" throope's 'agle to be sure, that we brought al the way frum de Platte! He wus a foine bird, loot'unt, so he was! He'd licked "C" throope's goat, an' he picked de oieye outen "G" cumpany's tarrier! An' now he's murdurhed!'

"'Is poor old "Grant" dead?' asked De Canter; showing sympathy for the old veteran, who had worn chevrons before he joined: 'What killed him?'

"'That bloomin' doughboy Loot'unt Thavisstock paid to massacree 'im wid de sthable broom, to be sure. Bad luck to 'im!'

"'Why did Lieutenant Tavistock want "F" company's eagle killed?' asked the innocent and unsuspecting officer.

"'To stuff de commissary baskits of them women from Fort Burns! poor old "Grant"! He masqueraded, sor, as a wild turkey an' they et 'im, they did! jist as pay day's cuming an' we was a goin' to pit 'im wid "K" throopes crower. Boo-hoo! But it was sport, loot'unt, to see the boys shling belting the doughboy outen the post! Be Gob, sor, he yelled loike a thayvin' Arrah-payho!'

"So Tavistock's outrageous deception was laid bare, to De Canter at the least! The old eagle which had been given by the 22d Cavalry in exchange for a lame monkey, and for some time had been recognized as the Sullivan pet of the regiment, had been placed before his guests, who had devoured him, fancying they ate wild turkey shot by their skillful and polite host! Yes; and De Canter recollected that he also had eaten of the National bird! 'Ugh!' he remembered now of having detected a peculiar flavor; but had said nothing lest he might betray his ignorance respecting swell cooking! And while McGoon drained in silence the unfinished glasses, the disgusted officer strolled away to reflect in solitude. But he was met by Lieutenant Curry, who gave him information which caused him still greater surprise.

"Curry told him that in an hour or so—after the guests had thoroughly digested their dinner, it was the intention of Tavistock—who fancied they were in the scheme with De Canter—to make a little speech. He would open by thanking them for coming; he then would apologize for the deficiency in the dinner by stating that he had received no knowledge respecting their coming until he beheld them in the garrison; that then it was too late to capture the promised turkey, so he did the next best thing by appropriating a National bird, which, though an old pet in his troop, he regarded as a fit subject to dissect on a National holiday, etc., etc.

"Tavistock was certainly in a position to crow!

"'The infernal scoundrel!' exclaimed De Canter, realizing the extent of his host's depravity, and fully conscious that a portion of old 'Grant' was sticking to his ribs; 'why, it will be a disgrace to the regiment, if not to the corps!' Then turning to Curry, he said: 'I can't thank you enough, old man, for having told me this; I'll balk the beggar yet!'

"And together they went to Tavistock's quarters, where the visitors and others were pleasantly conversing. A few moments later De Canter—who had never addressed an assemblage since the time he stood upon the platform and told his schoolmates the thrilling story of the heroic boy and the burning deck—arose and said:

"'*Ladies and Gentlemen:* I am conscious that it is bad form to trumpet one's own deeds; but I feel it my duty to inform you of a dastardly plot, of which you were to be the victims; which was frustrated by my interference!'

"(The company express gratitude and surprise, and Tavistock pales.)

"'It appears that Mr. Tavistock regarded your presence here to-day as part of a scheme to embarrass him. It is only proper for me to add that when he invited you to dine he had no hope of your coming. But he eventually learned you would be here, and satisfied that it was a trick to annoy him, and realizing his inability to provide the promised dish, he sought to turn the tables upon you!

"'Through the instrumentality of a wretch, who I am

thankful to say is no longer in the garrison, he had the old pet eagle of " F " troop killed and placed before you to pose as his wild turkey !' (Cries of ' The monster !' ' The beast !' and various sounds which show the paucity of orthography.)

" ' Yes, ladies and gentlemen, and it is his belief at this moment that the bully of " F " troop has been devoured by you! But when I learned of his purpose, I quietly sent the turkey which was to grace my own modest board over to Mr. Tavistock's cook with instructions to prepare it properly for you, and to decently inter the dead champion of " F " troop. From this you will perceive that it was my precaution alone that rescued you from a fate too hideous to contemplate.'

" It seems needless to add that De Canter stock instantly rose in proportion to the decline in Tavistock ; and though the lie told by the former was far too dark to be classed with the ' white ' ones, it completely foiled the latter, and prevented sudden and serious illness among the visitors."

" It is time we heard from one of our guests," said the Colonel ; " local talent isn't exhausted, but these fellows, like the poor, we have ever with us. Come, Major Loomis. You told the best story I ever heard, one night when we were camped at Warrenton, in '63 -- "

" Yes, yes, Major Loomis," impatiently called a dozen voices.

" But my yarns are all blood-curdlers," said Loomis, gravely. " The story Colonel Grace refers to was of the supernatural nature, and I had happened to be so placed as to have to hear a good deal of that sort of thing some years ago.

" I dote on ghost stories—and Mr. X. was such a sell," pleaded the lady with those effective eyes.

"Tell us one. Tell us anything, Major," came from the table generally.

"Well," said he, "it needs a yarn like one of mine to bring things to a rational temperature after hours of such delight and festivity. List—list—oh, list—

THE MAJOR'S STORY.

"The more we are brought in contact with the known forces of Nature the more we become impressed with the fact that there are subtle influences exerted by them on the human system. Many occurrences which, in this century, we know are the result of contact with these known forces were, in the last century, accorded to ideas generated by superstition. While, therefore, enlightenment throws a mantle over superstition, education seems to have lifted the veil of spiritual matters to such an extent that we no longer attribute to legerdemain the Mesmeric power; but are compelled to admit that there are those who possess in a high degree the power to enslave the human mind, and bend its every action to the vagaries of that power.

"That there are persons who possess the gift of what is known as 'second sight,' we do not for one instant doubt; but what force is exerted upon the mind to produce these glances into unknown mysteries has never yet been discovered. We can only accept facts as they appear.

"Captain Charlie Calverton, formerly of the —th Infantry, was a warm personal friend of mine, and a bachelor, somewhere in the neighborhood of fifty years of age at the time of which I speak. I was visiting him a few years before his death, at Fort Blanco. While at the post

4*

a large dancing party was given, and, of course I, with my host, attended. During one of the dances I was seated near two ladies with whom I, at intervals, conversed. At a lull in the music one of them turned to me and observed—

"'Major, I believe you are one of Captain Calverton's oldest friends?'

"I admitted the fact, and paid some complimentary tribute to his loyalty.

"'Well,' said the lady, 'we have often wondered why he has always remained a bachelor. He seems so deferential to women, and apparently is pleased with their society; he loves music, yet I have never known him to dance; and he has a singular fondness for all kinds of flowers—that is, if I except heliotrope? Perhaps you can solve the riddle for us?'

"'Why do you say that he loves flowers of all kinds except heliotrope?' I queried.

"'Because he cultivates them whenever he has the opportunity; but amid the endless variety that I have known him to have I have never seen the flower mentioned; and to convince me that I was right in my surmise, I have seen him turn pale at the sight of it. On one occasion he was offered a *boutonniere* of heliotrope by a lady, and his rejection of it was really rude. You may depend upon it he was never tendered another flower by that lady.'

"I drew my own conclusions as to who the lady was that had been referred to, and therefore, to soften her feelings a little, I told her that the captain had some very painful recollections concerning a sprig of heliotrope.

"'Oh! then he has a history?' she exclaimed. 'Do tell us what it is; I'm dying to know.'

"She didn't look very much like expiring suddenly, so

I excused myself on the ground that the Captain's history was his own, and that I did not feel justified in saying more than I had said. But that night, after the Captain and I had gone to his quarters, and we were quietly enjoying our cigars, I alluded to the conversation, when he approved of what I had done, and at the same time requested me never to allude to his past life in the presence of others while he was alive. A telegram hurried me away the next day, and so I was saved the trouble of refusing the ladies a second time. But the Captain is dead now—gone to investigate mysteries over which we conversed for many an hour. His spirit is often with me. I'm not a spiritualist, either by faith or practice, nor can I account for the mysterious influence which causes me to feel a spiritual presence; but so impressed have I been with that belief that I have reviewed his whole life, and I have, for the first time, resolved to relate his singular history, showing a fatality about matters over which he could exercise no influence.

"There is a period in the life of all children when they begin to doubt the actual existence of the mythical personage known as 'Santa Claus.' Forty-five years ago this mysterious giver of all good things was a veritable individual in the minds of children for a longer period than at the present time. Hence it was that Master Charlie Calverton, who had arrived at the sublime age of eight years, had been kept in ignorance as to the identity of the generous patron of Christmas day. This may have been caused by several circumstances, for the largest towns he had, up to this time, seen, were those of the straggling village of Washington City, containing about 40,000 inhabitants, and the shipping port of Alexandria, Va.; and this experience had been confined to a single visit of a few days to each of those places, for his home

was in one of the lower counties of Maryland, bordering
on the Potomac River. The facilities for communicating
with the outer world were very meagre in character at
the time referred to.

"But at this particular period of young Calverton's life
he began to have his doubts about Santa Claus, and had
learned from a primary geography, in which he was being
instructed, that the earth was supposed to be 25,000 miles
in circumference. He therefore asked his father one day
if there was only one Santa Claus, to which he received a
reply in the affirmative. His next question was : ' Then
how can he travel so many miles in one night, and visit
so many houses ? '

" This was somewhat of a poser for his father, who did
not wish to destroy the pleasing fancy of childhood. So
Charlie was told that Santa Claus had reindeer as swift as
the wind. He had never seen a reindeer, and therefore,
trusting to his father's superior knowledge, he made no
more inquiries. But as Christmas drew near in this, to
him, ever memorable year of 1845, from little remarks
that he had overheard among his elders, his doubts returned in full force, and he determined that he would see
Santa Claus with his own eyes, even if he had to lie awake
all night.

"In order to have a clear understanding of events
which took place, it will be necessary to give a description of the home where Master Calverton first saw the
light of day, and where he was living at this particular
time. The mansion was quite unimposing in character,
although somewhat imposing in dimensions. It was a
kind of rambling frame structure, the central portion of
which, like many other Southern houses, was two stories
in height, with portico and large white pillars in front,
while the remainder had been built at different periods,

as its succession of occupants had seen proper to erect additional rooms, without symmetry, and with no view to architectural beauty. It was a sharp-roofed building, just affording space enough for several sleeping apartments above, while as many chambers below were allotted for the same purpose. It was in the midst of a square lawn, of rather large dimensions, around which towered great Lombardy poplars, while extensive beds of beautiful flowers of all descriptions cheered the eye with their variegated hues. Some fifty paces from the front row of poplars ran the shallow waters of Silver Creek.

"An immense hall ran through the centre of the house, on the left of which, as you entered, were three rooms, the front being used as a family sitting-room, while that immediately in rear of it was the bed-room of Mr. and Mrs. Calverton. The third was built as an addition on the side, and communicated only with the sitting-room. This latter was occupied as a chamber for Mr. Calverton's two children, Charlie and Joe.

"Christmas eve came. The boys' stockings, as well as those of the parents and the domestics of the house, were, as was customary, fastened to the sitting-room mantel, and the entire family had retired to rest. From the position where Charlie lay, tucked up in the bed-clothes, could be seen the row of stockings, and while awaiting the advent of Santa Claus he counted them over and over again, until it seemed to him there were hundreds of them.

"He had watched the flickering flames make their last leap into the wide-mouthed old chimney—had seen the glowing embers in the fire-place die out one by one, and was thinking he had imposed upon himself a useless task, when, suddenly, the room became illuminated as if by a thousand candles, and as his eyes expanded with aston-

ishment, a human female form rose up as if from beside
his bed, and rushed through the open doorway into the
sitting-room. Charlie had always been considered a
brave little fellow, and though terribly frighened, jumped
from his bed, thinking that if Santa Claus came in that
manner a wonderful discovery would be made, and he
would have the pleasure of relating how he had caught
the old fellow in the act. He therefore followed the glaring figure into the room. As he neared the centre he
gave one shriek and fell senseless to the floor.

"His piteous cry awakened both father and mother,
who hastily sprang from their bed, and while the father
was engaged in lighting a lamp, the mother hurried
through the dark to the bedside of her children. Finding
that Charlie was missing and that Joe was asleep, she
returned to the sitting-room just as Mr. Calverton brought
the lamp, and there they discovered their senseless boy.

"'What could it mean?' 'What was he doing there?'
These were the questions that father and mother naturally asked each other as they raised their little boy from
the floor, and endeavored to resuscitate him. But no
reply came from those childish lips. Charlie lay in a
death-like swoon, and the pulsations of his heart could
scarcely be distinguished. A man-servant was called and
dispatched for the doctor, who lived only two miles away.
In the meanwhile the mother exhausted all her ingenuity
in her applications for restoration. In the course of three-
quarters of an hour the doctor arrived, and after having
been informed of what had occurred, he commenced his
treatment of the case, succeeding so far that in a short
while they had the satisfaction of seeing Charlie open his
eyes; but upon discovering again a bright light in the
room, shuddered as with an ague and quickly closed
them, apparently relapsing into his swoon.

" ' What is it, my son ? ' asked Mrs. Calverton. ' Mamma is near you—nothing can harm you. Tell me, my boy, what is the matter ? '

" After repeating these words several times, while bending over his prostrate form, Charlie again opened his eyes, and throwing his arms about his mother's neck, exclaimed, ' Oh, mother.'

" This was all he could say, and the doctor advised that they leave all questioning alone until morning. So the little fellow lay with his arms about his mother's neck until sleep overcame him, when he was again placed in his bed, while the mother watched beside him during the night. At intervals his little face would warp as with pain and his body tremble from head to foot.

" When he finally awoke, some time after daylight, and was questioned by his mother, he said : ' I was watching for Santa Claus and thought I had found him, when I discovered it was a lady all on fire, and she uttered such awful cries, and was burning up so, that it scared me nearly to death.'

" Mrs. Calverton tried to convince her son that he had been dreaming—that no one had been on fire and that there was no lady in the house but herself, so that he must be mistaken. But Charlie insisted on it that he was wide awake and saw everything. No one could conjecture what it all meant. The father argued that the boy had been troubled with a bad dream ; the mother was not so well satisfied, as she had never known him to walk in his sleep ; while the old negro cook said : ' Dere's gwine ter be sumpin' tur'ble happen—Mars' Charlie's done got secon' sight.' There was one thing certain—Charlie never watched for Santa Claus a second time, nor could he ever be prevailed upon to sleep in the same chamber.

" The sunny days of childhood passed only too quickly,

and when Charlie arrived at the age of fourteen years both boys were sent off to school at Baltimore. At the end of three years Charlie was appointed a cadet at the West Point Military Academy, while Joe continued at school for two years longer, and finally entered college.

"Charlie graduated in due time, and after spending his three months' furlough at home was assigned to a regiment then doing duty on the Indian frontier. But the winter he spent there was harassing in the extreme, on account of the secession movement, and he was actually glad when war was declared, and he was ordered with his regiment to the East. This gave him the opportunity of paying a visit to his home, although he ran the risk of being captured by the enemy, who occupied the lower Potomac at this time. Mr. Calverton had strong Southern proclivities, but his wife was equally strong in her support of the Union, and thus matters at home were kept upon a neutral basis. The result, however, was that Joe adopted the father's side of the question, and hastened to join the rebel army; while Charlie, although urged by his father to either go South or stay at home, never for an instant flagged in what he considered his duty to his country. Thus it was that the brothers were arrayed one against the other, while the mother's heart was torn with anguish at the thought. With bitter upbra'dings from his father, and with blessings from his mother, Charlie left home to take his place in the Army of the Potomac, and to participate in the greatest struggle that any nation has ever been called upon to endure.

"During the Antietam campaign he received news of the death of his father, but it was not until the armies were confronting each other before Fredericksburg that he could get away, and then only for a few days, he simply having to cross the Potomac River. His mother begged him to resign and stay at home; but he argued that it would be cowardly to do so during hostilities, and a battle in prospect. He assured her, however, that as soon as the war was over he would tender his resignation and devote his life to her.

"The day before he left for his station he came into the breakfast-room looking pale and haggard, seeing which, his mother inquired if he was ill, or if he had passed a restless night.

"'I am not ill, mother,' he replied, 'but I have passed a restless night—all in consequence of some peculiar sensations that I had before going to bed. When I retired to my chamber last night, I sat by the window smoking a cigar and watching a few filmy clouds that were passing rapidly over the moon's face. Suddenly my mind became fixed, as it were, and there opened before my vision a beautiful stretch of country that I had never seen before —a lovely valley between two prominent ridges. All about me were fields of grain, green meadows and ripening orchards. I found myself standing with an army on one of these ridges. Presently a great roar of artillery reached my ears, the clash of arms resounded, and amidst the din we moved forward down the slope and across the beautiful valley. Then a great cloud seemed to envelop everything. But, in a little while, a rift occurred, and while I was watching it I saw father, as plain as I ever saw him in life, stretch forth his hands, and in another moment I saw brother Joe running to meet him with outstretched arms. In an instant he was drawn to father's breast; and while they stood with arms locked about each other the rift in the cloud closed and obscured them from view. I called to them several times, and then the cloud broke again; but this time father and Joe were moving forward, arm-in-arm, with eager expectation on their faces. I called again, but they paid no attention to me. Suddenly, out of the cloud on the other side of the rift, you appeared, with a most radiant smile on your face, and rushed into father's arms. Then all became black. With the perspiration standing in great beads on my forehead, I recovered from the mysterious spell with which I had become transfixed, and saw that the clouds had gathered in masses, and that the moon was peeping through a rift in them. I tried to convince myself that it was a dream, but it was of no use, and so I lay awake nearly all night.'

"'It was but a dream, however,' said Mrs. Calverton, 'caused by your watching the clouds. Of course it can mean nothing, my boy. Do you remember what a dream you had about Santa Claus when you were a child? Nothing ever came of that.'

"'That is true,' Charlie replied; 'and I trust nothing will ever come of this, but I cannot rid myself of the influence.'

*   *   *   *   *   *   *   *   *   *

"It was the 2d day of July, 1863. Night had thrown her mantle around the bullet-scarred face of the 'Round-Top,' and over the shell-plowed furrows of the 'Peach-Orchard,' through which the serried columns of both Union and Confederate armies had successively charged that day, leaving the blue and the gray intermingled on the battle-field.

"The last boom of the brazen gun had died away upon the summer air; the last sharp crack of the rifle had been heard, and the hostile armies that had confronted each other on that fatal field of carnage—Gettysburg—were lying peacefully sleeping, many of their members never to awaken until the reveille of the resurrection arouses them from their slumbers. The wounded lay there, looking up at the bright stars of heaven; some wishing that death would end their miseries, and others fondly thinking of their homes, wondering if they would ever see their loved ones again. Mysterious-looking objects in human shape were darting here and there through the Peach-Orchard, flashing every now and then the light of lanterns on the prostrate forms lying there in the starlight. These were the surgeons and their attendants of the Union army seeking out their wounded and having them removed from the field. One of these flashes fell full upon the face of a fine-looking fellow dressed in Confederate gray, and one of the attendants remarked : ' Well, he's a handsome corpse.' The words were no sooner uttered than the individual referred to opened his eyes and asked for a drink of water. Certainly they would give it to him, for no animosities exist between brave men when they are placed *hors de combat*. One of the attendants stooped down and raised the poor fellow's head while another applied the canteen to his lips. After taking a long draught, the wounded man said, as his head was again placed upon the sod : ' Thank you ; I can die comfortably now.'

" ' Are you so badly wounded ? ' asked the doctor.

" ' Mortally,' he replied.

" ' It may not be as you think,' said the doctor, proceeding to examine the wound. But in a few moments he shook his head and said : ' I'm afraid it is all up with you, my boy. You can't live an hour. It would be causing you useless pain to move you. Is there anything you would like me to do for you—any message you would like to send to your people ? '

" ' Yes, doctor, thank you ; I have a brother in the Union army, and if he can bury me so that my body might be recovered and taken home to Old Maryland— to the old place—I would like him to do that much as the most he can do for me now. His name is Charlie Calverton, of the Regulars.'

"'My God!' came in solemn tones out of the darkness, a few yards away; and as the doctor turned to ascertain from whence the sound proceeded, the voice continued:

"'Doctor, doctor! come this way, please; I am Charlie Calverton!'

"It was but a few moments before the blue and the gray were lying side by side—Charlie with a leg fractured above the knee, and his brother Joe with a mortal wound through the abdomen. Charlie slipped his arm under Joe's head and drew it to his bosom, and there, while the summer breeze whispered a requiem, the two brothers, who, but a few hours before, had been arrayed against each other in mortal combat, breathed a last loving farewell on earth.

"Having placed the brothers together, the doctor left them alone, promising to come back. He then proceeded with his attendants on his dreary rounds. When he returned Joe's spirit had taken its flight. He could not bear to separate them, and therefore the dead and the wounded were taken together from the field to the rear of the Union army, where the final separation had to take place—Charlie being placed in the hospital and Joe buried in a spot that was marked by the doctor.

"The news that reached the old Maryland home from that dreary field, through the press, shriveled the mother's heart with a mighty sorrow, and prostrated her on a bed of sickness, during which time she wrote to an old friend in Baltimore—a Mrs. Meredith—to come to her in this her hour of extreme trial. Mrs. Meredith promptly obeyed the summons of her friend, and took her daughter, Nellie, along. The latter had just returned from completing her education at Boston, and was glad of the opportunity thus offered for a little country life.

"After the armies had disappeared from the field of Gettysburg, Charlie Calverton was removed to a hospital in Baltimore, and subsequently transferred to the hospital for officers, at Annapolis, from which place he wrote to his mother, giving her an account of the sad affair at Gettysburg, and informing her that as soon as he was able to get about he would obtain a leave of absence and visit home. Upon leaving Gettysburg he gave an accurate description of Joe's grave to an undertaker, and directed the body to be embalmed and expressed to his mother's house, where it arrived in due season, and was interred in the family lot.

"One bright, balmy day in the early part of September found Charlie on crutches at the door of the paternal mansion ; but instead of his mother to greet him, there was a strange lady. Beside her was a picture of youthful loveliness, such as Charlie thought he had never seen before. She was dressed in a costume of simple white, with masses of dark-brown hair forming a coronet to the beautiful face. Lieutenant Charlie Calverton, U. S. A., was from this moment a captured individual. He was warmly welcomed both by Mrs. Meredith and her daughter, and at once conducted to his mother, who was still an invalid and confined to her room.

"After mutual embraces, and many inquiries regarding the death of Joe, Mrs. Calverton observed—'Now that I have you again, Charlie, you must never leave me ; you must resign, and come home to live. I will not be long on this earth.'

"'Dearest mother,' said Charlie, 'I will stay with you as long as I can possibly do so ; but it is doubtful if my resignation would be accepted at the present time. The

Government is straining every nerve to secure men. See what New York City has had to undergo during the past month on account of the riots produced by the draft. As soon as the war is over I will return home and remain with you all my life.'

"'Ah, my dear son,' she languidly replied, 'it will all be over with me before the end of the war, and I feel the necessity here of your strong assistance.'

"'But, mother,' he added, 'you are feeling weak and sick now—you will be better after awhile, and then we will think about what you desire. Until then say no more about the matter; I am here, now, and here I will have to remain until I can get about on my pins again.'

"'Very well, my dear,' she replied, 'I agree to your proposition. Now give me another kiss, and go to your room and make yourself presentable, for there is a very lovely girl here whom it will be pleasant for you to meet.'

"'I have met her already, mother, and, do you know, I have fallen desperately in love?'•

"'Indeed!' exclaimed Mrs. Calverton, elevating her eyebrows; and then, as her son passed out of the room, she said to herself, 'I trust it may be mutual;' for, after having seen Nellie gliding about the house like a fairy for the past two months, and heard her joyous ripples of laughter, she could not but think that the charming girl would make her son an excellent wife.

"When the family met at dinner that day Nellie Meredith was more charming than ever, and in her beautiful costume of white lace was, to Charlie Calverton's eyes, perfection itself. As they arose from the dinner-table a white rosebud dropped from the flowers fastened on Nellie's bosom, and Charlie quickly picked it up, saying, as he did so, 'May I keep it?'

"'No,' she replied, adding, 'it is not worth keeping.' Then taking a sprig of heliotrope from the other flowers at her bosom, she presented it to him, saying, 'This is my favorite flower.'

"Mrs. Meredith remained with Mrs. Calverton for several weeks after Charlie's arrival, but, as she saw that her friend was steadily improving, she finally took her departure with Nellie—Charlie having, in the meanwhile, availed himself of every opportunity to enjoy the beautiful girl's society. In fact, he had become deeply in love with her, but had advanced no further in making known that fact to her than obtaining permission to call her Nellie.

"Thus matters stood in the month of April of the following year, when Charlie felt that it was time for him to report for duty with his regiment, his mother having apparently recovered her health, and his fractured limb no longer giving him trouble. After much opposition on the part of his mother, he proceeded to Baltimore, determined to see Nellie Meredith before he took the field; but at the same time resolved not to make known his love until he could ask her hand in marriage. He therefore stopped at a hotel for a few days, although the Merediths urged him to remain with them, and paid daily visits to Nellie. It was the night before his intended departure from the city, and having bade the family good-bye, Nellie accompanied him to the front door.

"She stood in the doorway like a framed picture, and in the bright moonlight which flooded the front of the house, her loveliness was plainly to be seen. The form, dainty and small, was set off by an evening dress of pink, of some gauzy material. A fine white Shetland shawl, which should have covered the shoulders and protected them from the dews which were beginning to fall, had dropped away and exposed to view the exquisitely moulded form. Her face was upturned to the evening sky, in which Charlie discerned an air of wistfulness, almost amounting to longing. The contour of it was delicate; its beauty was of an order rare and peculiar. Large, luminous and star-like were the dark eyes. The complexion was of a clear olive, with just a shade of coloring, which gathered into the deep crimson of her sweet and tender lips. Great masses of dark brown hair were drawn back from the pure and perfect face, and arranged in coils around the head.

"As Charlie stood beside her he feasted his eyes on her loveliness; in a moment he held in his own the dear delicate hand. How tiny it looked, with the dainty ruffles of costly lace almost covering it! His heart beat so quickly that for a moment he could not speak. The subtle, nameless influence of the scene and hour was upon him; he was longing to take the small form into his arms, to press fond, lingering kisses upon the sweet crimson lips. After a minute's silence she turned her great dark eyes, filled with a soft, shy light, to his face.

"The innocent, child-like face, with its exquisite beauty. How strongly, how deeply it moved him! The wild love surging within him would no longer be put aside; it cried out, demanding satisfaction. Ardent, passionate words rose to his lips; it was with difficulty he controlled his emotions as to speak with a semblance of calmness. Holding her little hand tightly in both of his own he said softly, ' Nellie, I love you.'

"By the faint pale light he could see how the fast-coming blushes dyed the delicate cheeks—how the white lids, with their long heavy fringes, suddenly drooped over the glorious dark eyes.

"'I have loved you for a long time,' he said, bending

over the small form ; 'so dearly that I feared to trust myself in your presence, lest by word or look I might betray
my love.'

" Still the white lids drooped, and she shrank back a
little, where, in the shadow of the doorway, he could not
see her face so plainly.

" ' I dreaded lest I should betray my love, and so incur
your displeasure,' he continued.   ' I feared, too, that
your mother might be annoyed if she learned that I had
presumed to entrammel her daughter just as I was going
to the field ; and so I resolved to quit your house to-night
and try to conquer my love until such time as I could
offer you a home.'

" The little form shrank still farther back amidst the
shadowy dimness of the hallway.   Charlie followed.

" ' Nellie, it seems as though I had never known, until
this evening, the meaning of the word happiness—as if I
had never known before how fair was the earth.   The
flowers seem to have gained new beauty ; even the moonlight seems broader and brighter ; and all because I love
you.'

" A great silence reigned around them—he was growing desperate.

" ' Nellie, my love, my darling, can I dare hope that
you love me ? '

" But still she did not speak ; and hope, which beat so
high in Charlie Calverton's breast, now began to fade
away.

" ' My darling,' he pleaded, ' I love you so dearly—
give me some hope.'

" But not a word did she utter.   Hope died out then.
He released her hand with a heavy sigh and turned to go
away.

" ' Forgive me,' he said, ' if I have pained you.   Per-

5

haps you may think I presume, even if my mother does not think so?'

"He stood for a moment in the doorway. The moonbeams falling upon his face revealed its deathlike whiteness · its rigid, set expression of bitter pain.

"'Good-bye, Nellie,' he said; 'I pray that you will forget that I ever presumed upon your kindness.'

"He stepped out on the porch, never looking behind him. Wounded pride and love were making life seem a most undesirable gift to him just then.

"Then there was a rustle of fabrics, a little faint cry of 'Charlie,' and a tiny, trembling hand was laid upon his arm.

"Oh, the change that passed over his face—the joy that flashed into his gray eyes!

"'Nellie, my love, my darling," he whispered, as his arm stole about her delicate waist, and he bent over her to catch the faintest whisper from her crimson lips.

"'I love you, Charlie,' she murmured; 'I have loved you ever since I first met you.'

"He caught her in his arms and held her against his loyal heart—the dainty form he loved so well. He pressed fond, lingering kisses upon the warm lips that were now sealed to his own.

"'My life, my love, my queen,' he murmured; 'how I love you—oh, how I love you!'

"They stood silently, then, she nestling to his side as though there she had found her home. She was not a grand, dignified woman, this Nellie Meredith; she was simply a clinging, sensitive, innocent girl, with a nature which gave affection and craved the same in return. She loved Charlie Calverton, and the knowledge that he loved her so filled her heart with supreme happiness that her lips refused to speak until despair seized her at the thought of his leaving her.

" ' It may be years yet before the war terminates, Nellie,' he said; ' but at the end of that time may I claim you for my little wife?'

" ' Yes, Charlie, I will wait for you,' she replied, looking into his eyes and then kissing him fervently. ' There,' she said, ' that's the first kiss I ever gave to any man, and it is to seal my promise.'

" ' God bless and protect you, my own dear love,' he said, as he bent over her and took a last lingering good-bye kiss. And then he left her with his heart full of gladness—nay, unbounded joy—the remembrance of which consoled him during many a hard march and fiery battle in those uncertain days of '64, from the Wilderness to Petersburg. At the first opportunity he wrote to Mr. Meredith, telling him of his love for Nellie, and asking her hand in marriage as soon as the war was over. He received a very kind letter in reply, stating that if he and Nellie were of the same mind when that event took place, he himself would interpose no objection.

" When the army had settled down for the complete investment of Petersburg and the chilly days of winter had come, Charlie Calverton was once more called upon to witness the verification of his singular presentiment, for Mrs. Calverton's health rapidly declined on the approach of winter, and Charlie had barely time to reach home after receiving the news of her illness, before she passed over to the other shore to meet her husband and Joe.

" Charlie was now alone in the world—all the family gone. The old Maryland home was too full of sad associations, and therefore leaving it in charge of an overseer, he visited Baltimore and gave full authority to an agent to dispose of the property. It is needless to say that during the two days he was there he spent most of the time

with his charming *fiancée*, and then hurried back to his
regiment, to participate in the campaign of 1865.

*   *   *   *   *   *   *   *   *   *

"At last peace was announced, and one day in the
month of May Charlie started for the purpose of making
arrangements for his wedding-day ; but upon his arrival
in Baltimore he found that the family had gone to Lower
Maryland for the summer. Ascertaining their where-
abouts, he followed quickly, and upon his arrival was
astonished to find that they were living in his old home,
which Mr. Meredith had purchased from the agent, and
Nellie had purposely kept him in ignorance of the fact,
thinking it would be a pleasant surprise. And, indeed,
it was intended as such to Nellie herself, for Mr. Meredith had remodeled the house materially and furnished
it in modern style, desiring to present it to her on her
wedding-day. The first Tuesday in September was,
therefore, fixed upon as the day for the happy event, after
which they were all to return to Baltimore for the winter ;
but when that time came, and Charlie applied for a leave
of absence, the authorities declined to grant it, but informed him that he could renew his application after the
winter began. It was then decided that the family should
remain at the old homestead until after the Christmas
holidays, and the wedding take place on Christmas day.

"The holiday season came at last. The rooms formerly occupied by Mr. and Mrs. Calverton and the boys had
been decorated and furnished especially for the bride and
groom, and Nellie was occupying the boys' bed-chamber
already. Charlie had been at the house for several days.
Several friends of the family had arrived from Baltimore
and were attending to their own affairs. It was Christmas eve. The trousseau had all been prepared, and the
dressmaker, who had been summoned for the purpose

from Baltimore, was to see that everything was *en regle*. Nellie concluded that while the others about the house were engaged in their preparations for the festivities she would try on the wedding-dress, under the supervision of her mother.

"Accordingly she arrayed herself in her wedding apparel, and then sent for Charlie to come to the sitting-room and inspect it. Standing in the centre of the old room, he first admired his promised bride at some distance, exclaiming, 'How beautiful you are!' and then he gently drew her to his bosom and imprinted a loving kiss on her tender lips, saying, 'I love you! I love you—oh, so dearly!'

"As he released her from his embrace she stepped to a table that was loaded with flowers, and selecting a sprig of heliotrope therefrom, said:

"'When we first met, Charlie, I gave you a sprig of my favorite flower; now I give you another, darling, with the full force of all that its emblem implies—my heart's devotion.'

"He took the flower, kissed her again and again with a lover's fervency, and then she retired to her room, while he proceeded to pin the sprig of heliotrope to the lappel of his coat. He had barely succeeded in doing this when a scream of anguish, that rang out upon the frosty air like the wail of some tortured victim, reached his ears, and before he could realize from whence the sound proceeded, the bright happy being, who had left him scarcely five minutes before, rushed from her room enveloped in flames from head to foot. The maid had placed the lamp on the floor, the better to see how to unfasten her satin shoes, when, by some movement of hers, it was knocked over, the chimney broken, and the light, filmy drapery took fire. The girl lost her presence of mind and threw

herself on the floor.   Mrs. Meredith, who was sitting on
the other side of the room, sprang from her chair to ren-
der assistance; but Nellie rushed through the doorway
to the sitting-room for Charlie.   Regardless of himself,
he grabbed at the fire until his hair and eyebrows were
singed, and his hands and arms burned to blisters, while
she, suffocated by the flames, fell dead in the centre of
the room, the sickening flames lapping and hissing as
they charred the beautiful skin into blackened parchment,
at the sight of which Charlie Calverton fell on the floor
insensible.

"This is the reason why, twenty years afterwards, he
died a bachelor."

"We must have something to drive away the effect of
that.   Come! I have it.   *Place aux Dames.*   And who
can bring us back to sunshine better than she who
drove me to it?" quoth the Major, a moment later.
"Come, fair lady,—it is for you to speak," and he bowed
low to the blue eyes.   In an instant the table echoed the
appeal.   Pleas, objections, resistance—all were in vain.
At last the silvery tones of a woman's voice were alone
audible.   All others were hushed.

DACRE'S CHRISTMAS GIFT.

I. The Gift.

"Miss Dolly Devereux, aged sixteen, was the most in-
corrigible pupil in Madame La Pierre's 'select school for
young ladies.'   There were numerous others who, had it
not been for the dark background of Dolly's naughtiness,
against which their minor delinquencies were thrown out
white, by contrast, might indeed have been considered intractable; but her matchless depravity completely sur-

passed them all, and placed her on a pedestal quite alone. Who set pins in the kneeling-bench, upon the precise spot where the Reverend Dr. Dean's knees must press, as he prostrated himself in prayer in the school chapel? Who basely stole and secreted Madame's best wig the night she was invited to a grand dinner-party? Who personated a ghost, at the witching midnight hour, and frightened Miss Meeks, the teacher of mathematics, into violent hysterics? Dolly Devereux; and these misde-meanors was Dolly guilty of committing within the lim-ited space of two weeks, so that Madame's long-suffering spirit rose and boiled over to such an extent that Miss Devereux was (as she expressed it) 'rusticated,' and sent home for penitence and reflection before the Christmas holidays began. Patience had ceased to be a virtue, in Madame's opinion, and she had felt that it would be more than she could bear to tolerate the young vandal's pres-ence a day longer than was absolutely necessary beneath her roof. This punishment was received with aggravat-ing cheerfulness by the delinquent, who had not dared hope to leave the establishment for any vacation, however well merited and earned. She had been placed under Madame's care at the mature age of thirteen, or there-abouts, and there she had ever since remained, without once having gladdened the hearts and homes of her rela-tives and friends. Her mother, after a decorous period of widowhood, had wedded an army officer high in rank, when her only child was twelve years old; and, after a brief period, rendered lurid by the light of that weird child's presence in the newly-formed family-circle, a boarding-school in New York had been selected, and Dolly's young idea had been invited to shoot in a novel and unexplored direction.

"Now her school career was summarily ended (for the

present, at least), and she descended like a bomb-shell upon the hitherto comparatively peaceful household of her step-father, Colonel Everett Poppleton, at Fort Washington, Nebraska.

"It was the 14th of December when she arrived, and by the 18th she rejoiced in the acquaintance of nearly everybody on the post, was intimate with several, had befriended the laundresses, and made pets of the soldier's children. She did not believe in class prejudices in the army or out of it, she remarked nonchalantly to her step-father, having scandalized him by presenting a paper of peanuts to his immaculate and hitherto statuesque orderly beneath his very eyes.

"Colonel, or General Poppleton, as he desired to be called, spent his days in a maze of horrified incredulity, excited by his step-daughter's alarming escapades. Mrs. Poppleton speedily settled into a species of despairing resignation, while those outside, whom Dolly's follies and frolics concerned not, smiled leniently upon her, criticised her good-naturedly, and admired and wondered over her from a distance at which they felt themselves safe. She was, be it understood, a remarkably prepossessing young person in the trifling matter of appearance, with particularly guileless blue eyes, short baby curls of a golden hue, and a smile that could beguile the heart of the veriest cynic. Therefore it was only those unfortunate enough to be tied to her by the bonds of kinship, and thus able to regard her charms from an entirely dispassionate point of view, who found it possible to set Dolly down, once for all, as a being totally obnoxious. Indeed, to General Poppleton's alarm and astonishment, the new and unwelcome addition to his private family bade fair to prove an unexampled favorite with the members of his official family constituting the social life of the post. And in-

variably (*perhaps* it was a mere accident of fate) the
young lady selected as her 'most cherished' those persons in the garrison—unhappily numerous—who had
been so unfortunate as to come under the commanding
officer's ban.

"Lieutenant Oliver Renshaw, for instance, was on
'official terms' only with his colonel ; and of course his
sister, Mrs. Lansing, was, so far as General Poppleton's
family was concerned, also socially 'tabooed.' It was,
therefore, to those who had made any attempt at studying
Miss Devereux's character, a matter for no surprise, but
rather the contrary, that she should select the said Mrs.
Lansing as first confidante and friend. Indeed, she went
so far as to rave over the last candidate for her affections,
in true school-girl fashion, at home as well as abroad. '*Such
a beauty* !' she would cry, enthusiastically. 'The very
prettiest woman I ever saw, and with such charming
manners ! Only twenty-five, and yet a widow ; quite the
most *romantic* thing I ever heard. I only wish *I* were
twenty-five and a widow ; but I'm afraid there is no such
luck in store for *me* !'

"One afternoon she had entered Lieutenant Renshaw's
quarters without knocking, and had made herself very
much at home by Constance Lansing's side, while the latter
busied herself with some fancy work which was to be her
brother's Christmas gift. Miss Devereux had sat in silence
for a moment, having hopelessly entangled several skeins
of 'crewel,' and not being able as yet to think of anything more interesting to do. Suddenly she broke forth
in speech. 'I do wish I were an artist, so that I could
take your picture as you look now, with the firelight falling on your face and hair. Black is so dreadfully becoming to you, you know, with your beautiful, fair complexion ; but it isn't every one who is lucky enough to be a

5*

widow, and have an excuse for wearing mourning, you know.'

"Constance Lansing laughed. She had not cared for her husband, and therefore the tactless words found no sensitive place in her heart. 'My husband died three years ago,' she said, quietly, 'and I no longer wear mourning. But I am fond of black. It suits my fancy as well as my complexion.'

"'Just think!' soliloquized Miss Dolly. 'How nice it was of him to die while you were so young! as long as he *had* to die at all, you see. You don't look much older than I do even now, and I don't think of any reason why it should seem disrespectful if I called you Constance, do you?'

"'Certainly not. Call me so if you like, and if you don't find the name too hard to "come trippingly off your tongue." I am glad you take enough interest in me to wish to call me by my Christian name.'

"'Oh, *that*, of course. You know very well you are far and away the most interesting person on the post.'

"'Ah, you don't know everybody yet,' corrected Mrs. Lansing, shaking her chestnut head in a provoking way.

"'Why, yes, I do, long ago. At least everybody but that horrid Mr. Dacre, who shuts himself up like a hermit in his dilapidated old quarters at the end of the row, and who is going to be court-martialed next week. Serve him right, too, I dare say.'

"Constance Lansing's face flushed with a redder glow than the firelight had lent it. 'You are mistaken in thinking Mr. Dacre horrid, my dear,' she said. 'And it does *not* serve him right to be court-martialed next week. You shouldn't talk upon subjects you know nothing about.'

"'Hoity-toity!' ejaculated Miss Dolly, with more

force than elegance. 'I *never*, really ! But you don't mean to say he isn't a fiend after all? I might have known he was nice, though, just because General—no, *Colonel* Poppleton, I mean, says such hateful things about him every time he gets a chance.'

"'Your father hated him, I know,' said Constance. 'It is through General Poppleton principally that all his troubles have arisen.'

"'Don't call him my father!' cried Dolly. 'I'd be ashamed to own him as such ; and there is no reason I should, just because mamma happens to have changed a pretty name for an ugly one. But you have quite excited my curiosity, so do tell me what this trouble of Mr. Dacre's is.'

"'I scarcely know if I ought,' began Constance, doubtfully ; but Dolly interrupted her with a peremptory order to 'go on.' 'Well, the beginning of it is quite an old story now,—three years old,' Mrs. Lansing said, retrospectively. 'I remember it was just before I came here, after my husband's death. The whole regiment had newly arrived from Dakota, and Mr. Dacre had been quartermaster at his old post. In collecting property for the sudden move, a few articles were missing, for which he could not account. He knew they would be found afterwards, and he might have been able to account for them even then if he had wished to implicate another officer, but he did not. Of course he was responsible for them, at least according to General Poppleton. Finally, without going so far as to injure the other officer in question, he proved in a way satisfactory to everybody, except those prejudiced against him by his enemies, that the responsibility had passed from his hands, and he would not pay for the alleged missing goods. He said that to do so would be a virtual admission of his carelessness or guilt. The story is—but I must not tell you that.'

" ' Yes, yes ; I *insist!* I will know the rest.'

" ' The story is, then, that there are certain papers which have been " pigeon-holed " by General Poppleton that would throw a good deal of light on the matter, and the blame would be shifted to other shoulders than Mr. Dacre's. But, of course, that can never be proved, though most people believe it ; and, in the mean time, Mr. Dacre's pay has been entirely stopped for the last three years. He has very little to live upon, but has been braving it out, hoping for the vindication which has never come, and probably never will now, as this court-martial—if the charges are proved against him—may very likely end his army career. Poor, poor fellow! Such a bright, noble life marred and wasted?' The last words she spoke as if to herself, with a strange look of pain upon her fair face that passed unnoticed by self-absorbed Dolly.

" ' He really isn't horrid, then?' the latter queried, her head on one side.

" ' No.'

" ' And not old?'

" ' About twenty-nine or thirty.'

" ' Oh, that is not so *very* old—for a *man*. And is he good-looking?'

" ' He is called handsome. Here is his photograph you may see, if you like.' And going to her davenport, Constance took from a locked drawer a picture of a young man in uniform,—a young man with rather dark, smiling eyes, black hair, well-cut features, and an expression that was inexplicably fascinating, even beyond its evident candor and intelligence.

" Dolly examined it critically. ' I like him,' she finally

announced; 'and what is more, I am—going—to *call* on him.'

"'Oh, Dolly, *impossible!*' Constance cried.

"'You will soon find, my dear, that *nothing* is impossible with me. I am going to do it, as he is in arrest and can't come to see me, even if he cared to; and I am going this very afternoon. So, as it is growing late, I will say *au revoir*, which is about all the French I have brought away from Madame La Pierre's.'

"Constance looked at her young visitor aghast. 'You don't really mean that you will go alone to call on a strange man you never saw before in your life? Why, your father would never forgive you in the world!'"

"'Colonel Poppleton can attend to his own affairs, and I will to mine; but I say, would you like to have me stop in later and tell you how I enjoyed the call?'

"'Well, yes, if you are determined to go, and will not take advice. Just for the *curiosity*, you know, I should well enough like to hear what occurred.'

  *   *   *   *   *   *   *   *   *   *

"There were three chairs in the room, all old, with a suspiciously palsied look about their legs, and a depression about their seats which was apt to communicate itself to the minds of those unwary enough to trust themselves to their 'tender mercies.' There was a table covered by an ink-stained red cloth, a bit of carpet which looked like a small oasis in a desert of bare floor, a home-made book-case stored with well-worn volumes, and several good pictures on the walls. There were also plenty of pipes, tobacco-bowls, rifles, shot-guns, swords, stray newspapers and cobwebs, and in the midst of this desolation and confusion sat a young man clad in a uniform very much the worse for wear. But it was the best he had (although it had seen two years of nearly steady

service), and so he had no thought of taking time to
change it before receiving the visitor who was unexpect-
edly announced.   It had happened that Mr. Dacre's
'striker' was blacking Mr. Dacre's much-worn boots in
the back hall when the knock sounded, and so there was
some one to answer the door beside the master of the
house.   Indeed, the latter might even have invented some
pretext for excusing himself had not the visitor followed
the 'striker,' who had announced her name, to the door
of the front room.

" ' I was so afraid you wouldn't see me, Mr. Dacre, if
you just heard my name, and associated it with Colonel
Poppleton's, so I thought I would come straight in, and
you couldn't help yourself,' said Dolly Devereux's cheerful voice, as Dolly's pretty face appeared in the doorway
and lighted up the dismal room.

" Dacre was electrified.   It is possible that he had
never received a visit from an unchaperoned young lady
before, and the effect upon him was flatteringly pronounced.

" ' Aren't you glad to see me?' artlessly inquired
Dolly.   ' I mean to be very nice to you.   I have come on
purpose to be nice, and to cheer you up a little, because
people, and Mrs. Lansing especially, thought you needed
cheering up at Christmas-time.'

" ' Heaven knows I need cheering !' Dacre thought,
but he only spoke aloud the last words of the idea taking
shape within his mind.   ' So Mrs. Lansing sent you to
me?   That was very kind in her.'   And though Dolly
was pretty, undeniably bewitching, and dressed like a
grown young lady, he looked into her eyes, and knew
that at all events she had come to him only as a little
girl.

" ' No, she didn't.   She said I musn't do anything of

the sort. But she also said " Poor fellow ! Such a bright, noble life marred !" and she showed me a photograph she kept locked up in a drawer ; so I was interested, and came in spite of her, you see. And I mean to make your Christmas a merrier one than you think possible now. Oh, you don't know what I can do when I just *make up my mind* to it ! I suppose '—suddenly—' you quite understand who I am ? '

" ' I think so, Miss Devereux. Several people who have been so kind as to come and see me in my prison have spoken of you. And of course I appreciate your goodness in trying to give me a little Christmas cheer.'

" ' And you don't think I can do it ? '

" ' You can, if anybody could. But I fear I must wait until after next Wednesday before I can be beguiled into a very hilarious mood, and then the probabilities are, you know, that I shall be less inclined that way than ever before.'

" ' Next Wednesday ? Why, what happens then ? '

" ' It is the day set for my court. You see, they wanted to give me a little entertainment for Christmas-eve. I supposed you knew, or I would not have bored you by the mention of it, Miss Devereux.'

" Dolly rested her rounded elbow on the ink-stained table, and laid her chin in the hollow of her hand, while she turned a face full of interest and sympathy upon Mr. Dacre.

" ' It's a burning shame to have it Christmas-eve,' she exclaimed, ' when you ought to be thinking of hanging up your stocking. But won't you please tell me just what you are being tried for ? Honestly, I don't ask it meaning to be rude.'

" Dacre smiled in genuine amusement. ' Certainly,' he said ; ' but I doubt if you can understand. I won't go into the matter of charges and specifications, of which there are a good many, but tell you simply that I am to be tried for an alleged gross neglect of duty. It is imperative that an officer before leaving the garrison should ask permission of the commanding officer, while the lieutenant must also ask the same of his captain. And one officer of a company must always be on the post. Now, I went to town one evening, and my captain also was absent. A little trouble occurred among the soldiers while we were gone, and there was no officer of the company to attend to it. When we returned, Captain Clowser was called to account by the commanding officer (who, by the way, is a great friend of his), and said that I had never received his permission to leave the post. That I understood perfectly his intention of going away for the evening, and knew that I was expected to remain. I, of course, asserted that I *had* had Captain Clowser's permission to absent myself, and my words were construed as disrespectful to both my superior officers—so that was an additional offence. And thus it stands between us at the present time.'

"'Dear, dear!' ejaculated Dolly. 'How dreadfully it sounds! But, of course, you are not guilty?'

"'Of course I should be apt to say I was not,' returned Dacre, beginning to laugh; but, as he met her eyes beaming into his, a flood of sympathy, interest and candid trust, his whole expression altered suddenly. He was silent an instant, facing her, and then he said: 'No, Miss Devereux, I am *not* guilty of the charges. I am innocent, though I can scarcely hope that you will believe me, and I most assuredly do not expect my judges to believe me next week. I have everything against me—though I ought to have grown used to that in the last three years—and I think I shall be convicted and sentenced. It is my sole streak of luck to be alone in the world and have none to be injured by my fall. I have only fought against fate for the past three years, and perhaps the struggle may as well end now as any time.'

"'Yes, perhaps it may,' said Dolly, conscious that Dacre had been speaking more to himself than to her ; 'but there are different ways of ending things, you know. And oh, what a life I *shall* lead Colonel Poppleton, now I am quite sure of his being the fiend I have thought him all along ! He'd better be careful where he sits, steps, lies down, and what he eats and drinks after this, that's all *I* have to say, for he has got Dolly Devereux upon his track !'

* * * * * * * * * *

"It was Thursday, the 18th of December, when Miss Devereux paid her first call of condolence to her new protégé, and that call was not, by any means, her last. She, however, was not as general in her attentions towards her various friends in the garrison, and she saw far less of Mrs. Lansing than of old. As she had threatened, she devoted herself strictly to her mission, and the unfortunate General Poppleton's life was rendered a burden to him by salted coffee, sugared soup, mutilated newspapers and slippers internally ' set about with little willful ' pins and tacks. She also found time, however, for a very diligent study of army regulations—a book popularly supposed to be either beyond or beneath the appreciation of the fair sex —and might have been seen pondering deeply over the rules set down for the conducting of military courts. Sometimes she frowned, sometimes she smiled, and on one occasion General Poppleton was alarmed, but scarcely surprised, to find her executing sundry eccentric steps and pirouettes, indicative of exultation, all about the library, which once had been so sacredly his own.

"The principal ornament of this library was a large

and very beautiful mahogany desk, which had belonged (before Colonel Poppleton depleted his purse by purchasing it of Sypher) to a celebrated Russian countess. It was curiously carved and shaped to suit an elaborate system of secret drawers; and this mysterious article of furniture possessed a degree of fascination for Dolly that was positively painful. She became uneasy whenever she saw its proud possessor seated before it, and yet, whenever he was there, she managed to remain present also. One day she had ensconced herself with a book in the bay-window, and the heavy curtains had fallen between her and the twilight of the room within. She had become absorbed in her volume (which, by the way, was a naughty French novel, a remnant of the general's bachelor days, which had become stranded on that topmost of the book-case shelves, where the cream of such literature is generally to be found), and was not aware that any one had entered the room until, hearing a sound, she peeped through the aperture between the curtains, and saw her step-father standing at the fireplace, unconscious of the keen eyes dwelling upon his own.

" For a moment he stood with his hands behind him, in front of the fender, and there was a perturbed expression on his countenance which suggested to Dolly an explosion of the latest of her plots against his peace. What had happened now? she asked herself. Had he found the ammonia in his cologne-bottle? had he learned of the exchange between the ink and mucilage? or had he chanced upon the onions in his best civilian hat? Evidently, however, his emotion proceeded from matter exceeding even these in seriousness; for, going to the desk, he planted himself before it as if with a set purpose, and *then*—something which Dolly had long been vaguely wishing for took place.

He remained for some time at the desk, and the cuckoo inhabiting the Swiss clock over the mantel had appeared twice, announcing the hour and half-hour, before he rose and left the room. As the portière fell behind his stout form, Dolly laid her book down on the window-seat. Then she waited a moment, with a hand upon the curtain. The front door clanged unmistakably, and Miss Dolly ventured from her hiding-place into the fire-lit gloom of the empty room. She went straight to the desk, and seated herself in the chair lately vacated by the general. 'The first head to the left,' she said, half aloud, putting a plump little finger upon the nose of one in the row of small, carved, grinning faces that ornamented a panel on each side of the mirror set deep within the desk. She pressed firmly, with no result; then again, a trifle to the right, and the mirror swung aside, revealing a set of tiny drawers, one after another of which she hurriedly opened. In the lowest lay several long, folded papers, which Dolly glanced over with a rising color, and beneath them was a torn envelope addressed to General Poppleton, Fort Washington, and marked 'Personal.' Dolly looked curiously at the postmark, which was half gone, and would not have been able to make out the word with the meagre aid of the five connected letters 'Cheye,' had not a sudden recollection flashed into her mind. Oddly enough, she remembered hearing General Poppleton say the day before that he expected Captain Clowser to return from his business trip to Cheyenne in time for Dacre's court. This word, perhaps, then, might be Cheyenne,— and the letter? Yes, there was a letter inside!

"Now Dolly, dark as was the road of depravity which she had cheerfully traveled during the sixteen summers of her active life, had not been in the habit of tampering with the private correspondence even of her few enemies, and consequently she hesitated before inserting her thumb and finger between the torn edges of the envelope. But she did it at last, though the touch of the paper sent a tingling sensation through every nerve in her venturesome little body. 'I will just glance at the signature, at any rate,' she thought.

"'Howland Clowser' was the name scrawled along the foot of the second page of note-paper, and just above it were some words which Dolly's eyes fell upon almost—not *quite*—in spite of herself. 'Thanks for your assurance that you will see me through this affair, as you did through that unfortunate one three years ago. I shall stick to the line I adopted at the first, and do not see how Dacre can have the ghost of a chance. We will talk over the matter together before the court meets Wednesday, so that no discrepancies may arise.'

"Dolly's face flushed crimson as she read, or rather as these words forced themselves and their full meaning upon her consciousness; and without an instant's further hesitation she thrust the letter, envelope and bundle of papers into her little pocket, already crowded with girlish and innocent belongings. Then she slid the tell-tale mirror back into its place, and the whole appearance of the desk was as before. Equally deceiving was the expression of the pretty face, which by the time its owner had tied on her hat and sallied forth in the crisp evening air had assumed its wonted mask of youthful rectitude and candor. A very superficial mask it was on this occasion, however, concealing a storm of contending feelings, which vibrated between joy, triumph and remorse.

"The last sensation she had nearly managed to forget by the time she arrived at Dacre's quarters, and stood knocking (with a heart which beat as loudly as her knuckles) at the door. Dacre opened it himself, and threw away his lighted cigarette when he discovered his visitor's identity.

"'Isn't it rather late for you to be out alone, Miss Devereux?' he asked, when he had greeted her, and become convinced that it was her fixed intention to go in.

"'Oh, it might be if it were any one but me,' said Dolly, running before him into the house. 'Rules that apply to other people don't to me, as by this time you ought to have learned. I have brought the Christmas present I promised you at last.' Her voice trembled as she spoke, and Dacre instinctively felt that something unusual had occurred, although the lamps were not yet lighted, and he could scarcely see her face.

"'I didn't know you had promised me one,' said Dacre, smiling; 'but I am sure I thank you all the same.'

"'I promised *myself* to give it you, at any rate,' Dolly amended. "From the first day I saw you I vowed to do it if I could. I should have been glad to spite the colonel, even if it had not been that I liked you so much. I would have done this or anything else—for you. Do you remember what day it is?'

"'Yes,' returned Dacre, slowly and reflectively, staring through the twilight at the silhouette Dolly's profile formed against the window. 'Yes; it is the twenty-third.'

"'And to-morrow your court is to begin. Well, my Christmas gift reaches you just in time.'

"'You speak in riddles,' smiled Dacre, really puzzled by the girl's strange look and manner. 'But I must light the lamps, and do your gift the justice it deserves.'

"Dolly waited until the bare room was illumined, and then said, questioningly, 'Why is it, do you suppose, Mr. Dacre, that people who have done something wicked don't destroy all evidence against themselves, but keep enough put away secretly to tell the whole history of their crime?'

"'All that smacks a good deal of the ubiquitous dime-novel,' said Dacre, 'and it is more than I can do to explain it; but I believe it is generally admitted to be the case, queer as it seems. However, that has nothing to do with my Christmas gift, I suppose.'

"'Judge for yourself,' cried Dolly, with pretended nonchalance, as she handed Dacre a bundle of folded papers and the letter she had replaced in the envelope. For a moment he stood fingering them over in surprised silence; then his whole expression altered strangely, and his face flushed and paled.

"'What are these papers, and how did you come by them?' he questioned, in a strained, hard voice.

"Dolly became a little frightened, but bravely stood her ground. 'I watched my chance, and when I saw Colonel Poppleton put a letter in a secret drawer of his desk this afternoon, I waited till he was gone, and took it out with the rest of the papers that were there. Then I —then——'

"'Then what?' very sternly.

"'I—read them, and saw that, just as I suspected, they referred to you,—to your trouble three years ago, which Constance told me of, and also to this very court,—at least the letter does; and, oh, I was so glad!' She looked up at him half furtively, half appealingly, and was frightened at his face. 'Oh, Mr. Dacre!' she cried, 'don't be hateful to me about it! I can't stand it if you are, after all I have gone through for your sake. Don't scold me, but just think what you are saved from. There are the papers which fix all the responsibility of the loss three years ago upon Captain Clowser, and there is the letter which can prove to *anybody* your innocence in the case that comes up to-morrow. You will be a free man again ; the burden will be lifted that you have borne and fretted under for so long !'

" ' Good God ! that an innocent-faced child like you should prove such a temptress ! ' he exclaimed, staring at her with a species of horror growing in his eyes. ' Do you expect me to stoop to the basest dishonor in order to vindicate myself in the eyes of my world ? I would rather be dismissed the service to-morrow, with an undying stain attached to my name, than so much as draw that letter from its envelope, or remove the band that holds those papers together. I owe neither of the men you speak of any gratitude, but I would take no advantage of them in the dark. If their honor lay in my hands, I would give it back to them without exposing one stain, and fight my own battle in my own way, stand or fall.'

" He had spoken in a loud, excited tone, but his voice dropped as he concluded, and very quietly he laid the papers down on the table. ' I ought not have spoken to you so,' he said, turning to Dolly again with the expression which had frightened her fading from his eyes, and a strangely soft and pleasant light dawning there instead. ' I ought to have remembered your youth and inexperience, and how differently such matters must look to a child like you from what they appear to a man. You meant to serve me. You risked a great deal for me, and —I thank you, but you did not know what you were doing, and it remains with me to think for us both. Take those papers back—I can't touch them again : they seem to burn me—and put them where you found them. No one shall ever know of your Christmas gift, child, except yourself and me.'

" ' Oh, Mr. Dacre ! ' Dolly cried, ' you have se disap-

pointed me! I can hardly bear it. To think I have
done all this for you, and you will not accept it, but only
blame, and—and perhaps *hate* me for it! I wanted so to
help you, and now—you must suffer, and I can do nothing for you any more.' As she spoke bright tears rose
and glistened in her eyes, then rolled unrestrained over
her cheeks.

"Dacre went to her and took her hand impulsively.
'Don't fancy for a moment that I could hate you,' he
said. 'What I feel for you is as far as possible removed
from hate. You have been a very dear little friend to a
lonely fellow who has few real friendships to call his own.
But I think, when you reflect, you would rather have me
suffer than do a wrong, or even voluntarily profit by one
already done. And I shall never forget how you have
tried to serve me.'

"'There is yet one more thing I may do,' murmured
Dolly, through her tears.

II.   *The Court-Martial.*

As described in a letter from Miss Dolly Devereux to
her friend Miss Nettie Ainsworth.

"'DARLING NETTY,—When I wrote you last I was
very low in my mind. I scarcely know how to define my
frame now, but there is one thing, at any rate, I can tell
you. I don't see why people are always taking a woman
to represent an angel in pictures and stories. *I* think
now it ought to be a man, though, do you know, Netty,
men are awfully aggravating at times,—the very best of
them? They don't care if they break a person's heart!
But I must not stop to discuss questions in *philosophy*, as
I am sure you are pining to hear the conclusion of the interesting story begun in my last. It couldn't have been

more romantic if it had been all a *fib* instead of real honest truth, could it? and I believe you will say so, more than ever, when you learn the rest. Well, I wrote you on the twenty-third, the night Mr. Dacre refused to do what I wanted him to, and his court was set for the next day at eleven o'clock. I was desperate. I didn't care what I did. You know I had been reading all about that sort of thing in the army regulations (*such* a stupid book, my dear!), and I was confident there was only one thing for me to do, if I did anything more at all. It was an awful risk, too, and the bare idea of it gave me a feeling like little frizzles up and down my spine, while I didn't even know if Mr. Dacre, with his queer fancies about proprieties, would thank me for it; but I wouldn't stop to think of that. The court-room where he was to be tried was in a big house called the "headquarters building," and the hospital is in the same place. So I made an errand to get some medicine, and then slipped up to the court-room, which I had been in one day with an officer, just to take a peep. It was very early, and no one was there yet, which was just what I wanted, but my heart was beating so I could hardly think. I did what I had come for (what that was I will tell you by and by), and then I had meant to go out and come back again to sit in the room during the trial. Lieutenant Dean had promised to bring me, if I would wear a veil. But, just as I was ready to run, I heard some one outside the door, and I had only time to rush into a closet at the corner of the room without being seen, which would have spoiled it all. There were shelves full of books and papers in the closet, and I had to crouch down under them, which cramped me dreadfully, and, besides, I was afraid I should smother before I could get out. But even *that* would be better than having any one come in upon me

6

where I was. I was nearly frightened to death, too, on
account of spiders and other creeping things I quite knew
must be there. My head was high enough to let me peep
through the key-hole, luckily, and pretty soon the 'court'
began to come in. I wondered what time it was, but the
clock was where I could not see it, and nobody even
glanced towards it, so they must have felt very certain it
was the correct hour to meet. The officers were all in full
dress, and appeared quite solemn and grand. I could see
Mr. Dacre, and his face was white, but he was perfectly
composed, and had a brave look in his eyes that made
my heart beat fast. A colonel from another post was
president of the court, and I thought he seemed kind
and just—so different from Colonel Poppleton and
Captain Clowser, who came in as witnesses, and looked
(at least, to me, who knew *all*) ready to drop with
shame and guiltiness. By the way, I had had the fore-
thought to empty the red pepper-box into the colonel's
pocket-handkerchief before leaving home, so that when
he came to use it in the court-room he had a really terrible time, and I was afraid they would hear me laughing
in the closet ; but perhaps they thought it was a mouse.
Well, the trial went on, and every word was distinctly
audible to me. I felt like applauding, and shouting,
" Hear, hear ! " when Mr. Dacre plead " not guilty," in
a firm voice ; and then again I could hardly help running
out to choke Colonel Poppleton and Captain Clowser
when they told the pack of falsehoods they had skillfully
gotten up. Poor Mr. Dacre had no witness on his side
at all. His case had to stand on his word alone, and of
course that could not amount to much in the eyes of the
court against that of his captain and the commanding
officer of his post. It was an exciting trial, and the court
did not adjourn at lunch-time, but went straight on with

its proceedings. Once the court was "cleared," as they called it, when even the prisoner had to go out, and then the members talked about Mr. Dacre in a perfectly horrid way. No one but the president had a good word to say for him. So, finally, when all was done, and the court was "cleared for deliberation" for the last time, I felt quite prepared for what would come. They took a vote, beginning at the junior member, and every man (even that nice, kind-looking president) said "Guilty," without pausing for a moment's thought. Then they talked awhile, and presently each one wrote out on a piece of paper what in his opinion the sentence ought to be. At last one was decided on, which seemed to please everybody in the court, after they had discussed the fact of the prisoner's having already been in disgrace with the authorities during the last three years. He was to be dismissed the service of the United States, and the cold, cruel words made my blood boil within me when I remembered the uselessness and injustice of it all. But there was still hope, and now was the time to prove the success of what Madame La Pierre would call my *coup d'état*.

"'Just as the president finished speaking, a bugle-call blew outside the building. It was a call that every one there knew very well; and at Fort Washington it was always sounded at half-past three. The officers looked surprised to hear it, and those I could see glanced up towards the clock. Then I saw several take out their watches and stare at them.

"'"Mr. President," said one of the elder members, "this clock is much oo slow. We have exceeded the hour prescribed for the court, and the proceedings therefore become illegal."

"'The president pulled out his watch and glanced at

it, as though he could not believe the evidence of his own eyes.

" ' " This has been done purposely," he said, looking so very solemn and angry that I began to tremble and quake. ' This clock has evidently been set back by some person interested. It could never have so suddenly lost so much time itself.''

" ' " That, however, does not alter the fact that this trial will go for nothing, as all action taken after three o'clock, according to the order for the court, becomes illegal,'' replied the other man. '' And no officer can be tried twice upon the same charges.''

" ' Every one looked exceedingly blank, and I was so happy I forgot the cramps in my limbs that had come from so long sitting still.

" ' Just under the president's nose, on the big table around which they all sat, lay a volume of army regulations. Nobody knew better than I that it was there. He picked it up, almost as though I had mesmerized him into doing it, opened it where a lot of papers were put in as if for a mark—and of course he had to glance at the papers. They had been arranged with the writing outside, so he couldn't help seeing certain words, if he tried, and he *couldn't* see immediately to whom they belonged. That moment was the most trying one for me. I clinched my nails into the palms of my hands till they cut me, and the pain was almost a relief. But, oh, Netty! it all came right, and just as I had hoped and prayed, but hardly dared to think it would. When the president had read so far, he was bound to read more, and it was not till after he had learned too much to ignore that he saw the papers were private ones of Colonel Poppleton's. At least I suppose that must have been the way, for he started so that every one could notice it, and kept on reading, while his

face grew very stern and grim. Presently he said he had
just made a discovery that had a grave bearing on the
case in hand, and which it became his very painful duty
to take action upon. Then he stated what he had found,
and even told about the papers relating to the trouble
three years ago. Of course it would change matters
completely, he went on, and he would be obliged to lay
the affair before the reviewing authority. It would be
very serious for some persons concerned, but it was for-
tunate for Mr. Dacre that this had taken place in the nick
of time.

"'Well, that was virtually the end for that day; and
when the members of the court at last left the room, I
slipped out of my prison, feeling perfectly happy, but so
stiff and cramped I could scarcely crawl. I reached
home without being seen, but, much as I longed to, I
dared not go to Mr. Dacre with the blissful tidings of
what had occurred. I thought it would be better to let
him find it out in some other way. I went to Constance,
though, that same evening, when I found that I was positively *expiring* for a *confidante*. But, would you believe
it? she was just as unsatisfactory as she could be. Instead of hugging and kissing and crying over me, she
showed a feeling of jealousy on account of my success.
She was evidently very low in her mind when I went to
call, and when I told her the news, she would scarcely
credit it at first. When she did finally, she turned
ghastly pale, and looked ready to faint. And what do
you suppose she said? "And *you* have been able to do
all this for him—you, a child, almost a stranger, while I
—I have done nothing?"

"'I let her see that I was hurt, and couldn't resist the
temptation of remarking that, at any rate, *Mr. Dacre*
would appreciate what I had done, as he had already in-

formed me he valued my friendship. And do you know, Netty, when he said that, I wonder if he didn't mean *something more?* I am sixteen, you remember, and my dresses are quite to the floor.

" ' Now I must close, and shall add a postscript, with further developments, in a few days.

" ' P.S.—It is too bad I have allowed such an age to go by without finishing my narrative, Netty, but the truth is the times have been so exciting I have not felt able to write satisfactorily. This post has been exactly like a wasp's nest, and at home things have been especially *queer.* I have found out, however, in spite of all the mysteries, that Colonel Poppleton is going to resign, and I shouldn't wonder if Captain Clowser did the same. The inspector-general of the department has been at the house closeted with the colonel several times, and on each occasion the latter would come out after the interview with a smile the reverse of sweet. As for me, I am in awful disgrace, though of course no one knows positively what share I had in the affair ; and I am to be sent away to a horrible school somewhere in Boston (the very most rigid in that dreadful strait-laced place) I am informed. I shall sigh for Madame La Pierre's as for the " flesh-pots of Egypt," I'm afraid. It is now the twenty-fifth of January, and I am expected to be packed off almost any day. I dare say you are wondering at my running on in this fashion without a word of Mr. Dacre and my relations with him. But, oh, Netty ! I *cannot* bring myself to write at length on that subject. Boxes and boxes of candy could not make up to me for the disappointment he has caused me to endure. Not that he was unkind, or reproached me for what I had done. Oh, no ; when I saw him he thanked me in beautiful words almost as nice as men use in novels, and even kissed my hand as though

I had been a queen. He said, whether or not he approved the action I had taken, and it was too late to speak of that, he felt more grateful than he could ever express. I had given him back something far dearer to him than life—his good name—and now, when by an act of Congress he should be enabled again to draw his pay (thanks to me), he would beg leave to present me with the finest diamond ring he could find at Tiffany's, just to remind me continually of the gratitude which his best words would be too poor ever to make me understand.

" 'That was all very lovely, of course, but I expected it to be only a preface to something more ; and, would you believe it, Netty ? it *wasn't* that in the least.

" 'It is only a month since Christmas, and since he came out of arrest, but he has been at Constance Lansing's every day regularly, and now they are said to be engaged. I am even informed that he has been in love with her ever since they first met, though he would not ask her to marry him on account of his misfortunes ; but *that*, at all events, for my own vanity's sake, I shall try not to believe. I shall endeavor to think he really did care for me, but on account of Colonel Poppleton did not dare "ask for my hand," as the people say in story-books. And oh, Netty ! he is my *first* love, except Jimmy Allen and Tom Hastings, whom now I *scorn* to take into account. Constance is very friendly of late, and can hardly pet me enough, but I do not care to go to her house as often as I used. And, Netty, I wish you would advise me. If you were in my place would you take his diamond ring.' "

The applause of the evening followed this fair lady's gracious effort, and then no man was given the floor until " Dot," " Dora," " Miss Grace," had been appealed to by every voice at the table. It was only after a world of coaxing that "The Colonel's Daughter" told her tale:

THE COLONEL'S DAUGHTER.

"In my class at Vassar there were two girls—cousins, and inseparable companions; one was very fair, and was the daughter of General Lennox; the other was a very brilliant brunette, with high cheek bones and small, snapping black eyes. She was the daughter of Colonel Lennox, a younger brother of the General, but her mother was a half-breed Indian. Both girls bore the strange name of Kiamush.

"I spent the Christmas holidays of my Senior year with them, for their parents were in New York at the time, and I learned all the particulars of the strange romance which invested their mothers' lives.

"It seems just like a story, and if the parties were not living I think I would embellish it a little and send it to some magazine. I will tell it now, with the versions I learned from the different members of the family all blended into one, so as to make it a connected tale:

"Many years ago, when the West was a desolate region, with but few settlements, and mainly peopled by the Indians, who were far from friendly towards the whites, Colonel Hartwell's regiment was stationed at one of our distant forts—a place surrounded with the beauties of nature, but in entire exile from any places of importance. He brought his young bride with him—a beautiful girl of eighteen, with blue eyes and a profusion of golden curls—and, as there were only a few other ladies in the camp, she was naturally the belle of the regiment. Her husband idolized her, and was very proud of the admiration she commanded.

"After two years of absolute happiness, notwithstanding the cold and privations of two severe winters, and several skirmishes with the Indians, in which the Fort had been attacked, the Colonel's wife died, leaving as a legacy to her husband a little, blue-eyed daughter, and the remembrance of her own sweet life.

"She had requested that the baby be called Kiamush, after her Indian servant, whom she had deemed perfectly faithful, and who had lived with her from the day she came to the Fort, and to whose care she must now entrust her little one. The chaplain had christened the child at the bed-side of the dying mother. With her own hands Mrs. Hartwell placed around her little daughter's neck a string of gold beads, which her own mother had put upon her when she was a baby. The chain was so long that it wound twice around the little slender throat.

"The Colonel was so broken down at his wife's death that he was never willing to see the baby, whose very existence he hated. She was wholly left to the care of the Indian nurse, and the people of the regiment almost never saw her. The winters were so cold and the accommodations so poor, that the officers' wives seldom attempted to remain a second winter in the desolate region, but betook themselves to the East before another set in. Several years elapsed, and the Colonel still refused to take any notice of his child, who the nurse always assured him was well and happy.

"After as long as furlough as was allowable it was announced at the Fort one day that the Colonel was about to return, and that he would not come alone. His rooms were arranged, the grim Indian nurse was seen going about looking more severe and stoical than ever, and the

6*

little six-year old child, who had been in such seclusion, was seen at a window or door peeping out, but was always summarily jerked back by her nurse. It was current at the Fort that Colonel Hartwell's daughter was lacking mentally, and therefore had been kept all these years in the background, and many pitied the new bride for the responsibility she must assume.

"In an old lumbering stage plying along the prairie towards the encampment came the Colonel again, bringing a bride to the Fort, which had been much improved the last year or two.

"'My dear,' he said to his wife, as familiar landmarks showed him that they were not far from their destination, 'I don't know what you can do with Kiamush. I really know nothing personally of my child except that she is well and her nurse says happy.'

"'Do you mean, Henry,' asked his bride, 'that you willingly have had nothing to do with her? I supposed your regimental duties were what had prevented your seeing more of her.'

"'I have never held her in my arms or even kissed her since her mother died,' he answered, gloomily. 'And I seldom see her; she is frightfully tanned and does not look like her mother or me. I fear you will have a very hard time with her and that crotchety old nurse.'

"'Never fear, Henry, I have yet to see the child whose love I couldn't win.'

"'Or the grown person either,' said the bridegroom, smiling; for a weight was lifted from his shoulders at the thought of such a guardian for his little neglected girl.

"It was late in the afternoon when the stage rumbled up to the hotel which served as post-office and variety store as well. Several of the officers were there to meet their Colonel and convey him with honor to the barracks, where the few ladies gladly welcomed the new addition to their circle, and with feminine accuracy instantly decided her age, and passed judgment upon her personal appearance.

"Colonel Hartwell did not intend that his wife should go to the nursery that night, but she insisted, though the old nurse grumbled and said that the child was asleep. Mrs. Hartwell, however, gained her point, as she always did, and together the father, who had so long neglected his child, and the new mother, who yearned over the little one, and longed to fill a mother's place to her, stood, candle in hand, beside the little bed.

"Long the Colonel gazed at the round, brown face, for she was apparently very much tanned. Her crop of short, dark hair was so unlike her mother's golden locks.

"'You see, dear,' he said, 'there is no resemblance to her mother; I am afraid she is going to look like me.'

"'We will hope she will resemble both of her parents in character,' said the bride, a trifle disappointed perhaps herself.

"The next day after breakfast the little Kiamush was brought to their room to assist at the unpacking and get acquainted. She looked sullen and obstinate, and refused to go to either her father or mother. But it was not to be wondered at, for she had lived six years of pitiful isolation, the nurse always having refused to let her play with the other children at the Fort.

"Mrs. Hartwell coaxed her to come, and held out a gaily-dressed doll and a bright picture-book, but in vain. She then decided to go on quietly with the unpacking and see if, after becoming used to their appearance, the shyness would not wear off.

"On the bureau lay a large silk handkerchief, with a

gay border, and a little coral necklace ; the latter was intended for Kiamush.

"Thinking that they were not watching her, she crept stealthily towards the coveted articles, looking behind her to see if she were watched. Feeling that she was still unobserved, she proceeded to array herself. The kerchief she put square over her shoulders, knotting the corners in front ; being unable to unclasp the necklace, she twisted it around her wrist. Then seeing some feathers in a box, she tried to arrange them in her short hair, trying the effect in the mirror, and muttering some words in the dialect of the Ojibways, although she could talk English after a fashion.

"Suddenly she saw that she was watched, and a defiant expression crept over her face. But her new mother said gently : 'That necklace is for you, dear, but it is meant to go around your little neck ; let me unclasp it.'

"Kiamush looked at her distrustfully, but the pleasant smile reassured her, and she stood gently while the chain was arranged.

"From the box which the Colonel was unpacking he had taken a violin and bow and laid them on the table. The instant his back was turned the child had the bow and tried to bend it into a shape suitable for an 'archer bold,' and looked about, as if seeking for an arrow, but finding none, cast it aside.

"Finally she took the doll, petted it, and, rocking it to and fro, crooned a little lullaby over it : 'Ewa-yea, Ewa-yea.' She then started for the door, calling her nurse, and evidently eager to show her her treasures.

"Leaving her safe with her nurse, the Colonel returned to his wife ; 'Ida,' he said, 'I have only myself to blame that Ki is so like a little savage.'

"'Living only with an Indian, it is not to be wondered

at,' she answered; 'and I can do but little with her until I win her love; but it shall be won,' she added with energy.

"Weeks elapsed, and Mrs. Hartwell found that her duties as step-mother were more arduous than she had imagined. She at last won the child's love, but yet she would constantly break out in some flagrant act of disobedience. If punished, as oftentimes was necessary, she always planned and executed some act of revenge,—once tearing to pieces an exquisite scarf which Mrs. Hartwell had been embroidering; another time she threw a bottle of choice perfume out of the window, and unfortunately it fell upon the head of the First Lieutenant, who stood beneath talking to the Colonel.

"They suspected that these tricks were at the direct instigation of the old nurse.

"Kiamush had had absolutely no religious training; for how could an ignorant Indian woman teach what she did not know herself? Kiamush had only some idea of a Great Spirit, who, she thought, made the tops of the distant forest trees wave to and fro in the wind, and who also sent the fierce thunder-storms. At times it actually seemed as if she possessed no soul; not merely that it was unawakened, but that there was nothing spiritual to arouse more than we find in any domestic animal. It did not seem possible that the sign of the cross had ever been traced in baptism upon her brow.

"One morning, after they were seated at the breakfast table, she appeared with the curly scalp of her best doll suspended from her waist by a cord; and at night she insisted upon sleeping on the floor instead of in her bed.

"The Colonel and his wife talked it over that evening, and feeling almost discouraged, they decided that some means must be taken to separate her from the old nurse.

They disliked to turn her away, for the first Mrs. Hartwell had been really attached to her, and the child was
also perfectly devoted to her.

"'There is a tradition,' said the Colonel, 'that one of
my ancestors married an Indian, and heredity is such a
strange thing that it may be some of her traits have descended to my child.'

"Mrs. Hartwell laughed. 'We might as well believe
that in some former existence Ki was an Indian Princess,
and that her soul has merely taken to itself another
body.'

"'But really,' said her husband, 'I was not jesting,
for in Colonial times my great-grandfather harbored some
Indians during one of the Indian wars, and they vowed
that none of their tribe should ever harm a descendant of
the Leonards. That part of the story I know is true, but
whether he married into the tribe afterwards or not I
can't say.'

"'Her nurse's influence would account for everything,
I think,' said his practical wife.

"One day the Colonel called Kiamush to him, and
asked to see her string of gold beads; she promptly held
up her little coral necklace.

"'Not that; your gold beads, I mean,' he had said.

"'I never had any,' she replied.

"The old nurse being questioned, said that she had
put them carefully away, as the string was broken, and
she feared they might get lost.

"Christmas-tide was approaching, and every day Mrs.
Hartwell took little Kiamush in her lap and told her the
old, old story of that glorious night in Bethlehem, trying
to incite in her a love for the Holy Child and His teachings. Day after day she talked to her on the blessedness
of living a true, pure life, with no secret sins or naughty

deeds to conceal. She told her in simple language of the pain it brought to ourselves, and to our conscience—that little light within us—and, what was still worse, that it grieved the Holy Child and our friends also.

"The stoical old nurse was usually in the room sewing and listened with keen interest, but never betrayed by word what she felt. One day, however, she gave utterance to a deep groan and left the room. The next day she could not be found; then a week elapsed and she did not return. Kiamush mourned her absence, for Christmas was nearly there, and she was to have a tree for the first time, and all the children at the Fort were invited to come; but she felt that it would be incomplete without the one she still loved more than any one else.

"Christmas eve came and Mrs. Hartwell put Ki to bed early, so she had had a good, long sleep before the cavalry trumpet sounded for the extinguishing of the lights. After that she seemed restless, and called her mother several times, saying she had dreamed the Christ-Child was coming. She was much excited and it was long before her mother could again quiet her to sleep. In the morning she awakened with the same exclamation, saying, 'He has come and brought nursie with Him.'

"At breakfast one of the servants told the Colonel that the old nurse had returned laden with such a roll of blankets that she seemed scarcely able to stagger under it. As the guard knew her he had let her pass.

"After breakfast Kiamush went back to her bed-room for some of the little gifts which had been in her stocking. A loud scream from her brought the Colonel, his wife and others to the spot.

"There on Kiamush's little bed lay a delicate child with a profusion of tangled hair on its well-shaped head and around its throat a string of gold beads. Crouching in the corner was the old nurse, thin and haggard, but defiant in expression.

"'What does this mean?' demanded the Colonel.

"She remained in the same position, obstinate and sullen, and the sternness of the Colonel prevailed nothing. But Mrs. Hartwell went to her, laid her white hand upon her shivering arm and said quietly, but firmly, 'You must tell me what this means.' Then with little Ki nestling in her arms she poured forth a rather incoherent story which was similar to Tennyson's 'Lady Clare.'

> "'Are ye out of your mind, my nurse, my nurse,'
>   Said Lady Clare, 'that ye speak so wild?'
> 'As God's above,' said Alice, the nurse,
>   'I speak the truth; you are my child.
> The old Earl's daughter died at my breast;
>   I speak the truth as I live by bread!
> I buried her like my own sweet child,
>   And put my child in her stead.'

"Similar, I say to 'Lady Clare,' but with this difference. When the nurse found that the Colonel took no notice of the baby, and that it was frail and likely to die, she had taken advantage of his absence one time to go over the mountain to her people and leave the Colonel's child to live or die as the Great Spirit should decide; and had brought back her own little motherless grandchild from its forest home; whose mother had died of a broken heart because of the desertion of her white husband.

"She had kept up the deception until hearing Mrs. Hartwell's teachings to Kiamush, but they had wrought upon her to such a degree that she could bear it no longer. So she had walked miles and miles through the great snow-drifts and brought back the lost child.

"The truth of the story was apparent, for the slumbering child, 'the little Christ-child,' Kiamush called it, was a perfect likeness of its own mother.

"The Colonel saw the same rosebud mouth, the long, dark eyelashes and golden hair, the delicate taper fingers and the small, perfectly-shaped ear, fitting close to the head; and when the noise awakened the real little Kiamush, the lifted eyelids displayed great baby-blue eyes, with a timid, shy little heart looking out of them. Of course she was tanned, and had been sadly neglected as regards personal care, but, nevertheless, Colonel Hartwell recognized his own child, the legacy which his young wife had left him, and which he had despised.

"He was too overcome to decide what would be a fitting punishment for the treacherous nurse; but knowing that his own shameful neglect was the chief cause, he ordered for the present she be put to bed after having some food, and Mrs. Hartwell saw, herself, that she was securely locked in. Then the new child, who seemed much frightened, was put in a warm bath, then dressed in one of her supplanter's white flannel night-gowns, and after drinking a glass of warm milk she fell asleep once more beneath her father's roof.

"The little Indian Kiamush was hardly willing to leave the bedside of the sleeper, but Mrs. Hartwell bore her off to matins, which the Chaplain was to say at eleven.

"The Colonel wished to remain to watch his child lest the old nurse might repent of her repentance and secure her again, and Mrs. Hartwell felt that his thoughts were naturally in the past, and in them she had no share.

"The news of the strange arrival of the Colonel's real child spread like wildfire, and soon every company in the regiment was discussing the wonderful Christmas news.

"After dinner the children all assembled at the Colonel's apartments to see the tree, to which they had been invited. The little stranger from the forest, dressed in one of Ki's little frocks, sat shy and frightened on Mrs. Hartwell's lap, almost too dazed to cry at the strange faces about her, as the officers' wives crowded around, and yet she looked every inch a little lady, for blood will show.

"It had been a strange, eventful Christmas Day, and the Colonel and his wife sat up late that night discussing the future of the two children, same in age and name. Mrs. Hartwell, having become attached to Kiamush in these weeks of teaching her and caring for her, wished to adopt her, but the Colonel was opposed to it, for he felt very bitter at the thought of her having so long supplanted his own child. Still his child could speak no English, and the little half-breed could speak both languages to a certain extent, and therefore would be a great help as an interpreter.

"They felt, however, that they need not decide that night.

"Before midnight a heavy snow-storm set in, and the drifts piled up about the fort, and towards morning the thermometer fell rapidly. The next day it was found that the old nurse was missing, although her door had been locked on the outside, yet she had escaped. Her window was open, and there was a print beneath where the poor, frightened creature had jumped into the snow; and then here and there, off towards the direction of the forest a few struggling footprints, which had not been effaced by the drifts. A search was made, the tracks were followed, and by noon the dead, frozen body was found partially buried beneath a snow-drift. Thus the question of punishment for her, and the question as to retaining the Indian child, were settled by a Higher Power.

" The little Indian was christened by the name she had always borne, ' Kiamush ; ' and now Mrs. Hartwell found heart and hands more than full with the care of two children so utterly diverse in character.

" The blue-eyed child could not speak her native language, and had had the bringing up of a savage ; the dusky, dark-eyed Kiamush, who bid fair to rival the fabled ' Minnehaha ' in beauty, could speak the language of both parents, but seemed to have inherited the character of some bold Indian chieftain. No ordinary woman could have filled Mrs. Hartwell's position ; but love, combined with that gentle firmness which always commands respect, conquered ; and at fourteen no more beautiful or well-behaved children could be found in the camp than ' Colonel Hartwell's twins,' as they were called.

" The little Indian was the mother's favorite, partly because the Colonel was so fond of his own beautiful child, and partly because she was such an interesting psychological study.

" She seemed to be forced to live more than the dual life of flesh warring against the spirit ; hers seemed to be a quadruple existence. There was the animal life of the Indian and its spiritual superstitions ; ever antagonistic to the mentality and spirituality which she inherited from her white ancestors ; and the education she received never wholly obliterated the diverse influences from her soul. There was at times an uncontrollable desire for the free life of the forest, for hunting, roving and other unfeminine pursuits. But her devotion to the mother of her adoption, and to the child who came to her the first Christmas in her remembrance, never faltered.

" At eighteen they returned from boarding-school to Fort Snelling, where their father was then stationed, and immediately became the belles of the regiment. Lieuten-

ant Lennox and his brother, Captain Albert Lennox,
were the favored suitors for the hands of the 'twins.'

"When the Captain asked the brilliant, dark-eyed
Kiamush to marry him, she replied proudly, with flashing eyes:

"'I am not the Colonel's daughter, and I am prouder
of my mother's tribe than of my father's ancestry; but I
love you and will follow you, if you are not ashamed of
my parentage, but if you are I would scorn your offer.'

"The Captain admired her more than ever after this
outburst, for he had been sought after by the fair sex from
his cradle upwards, and it completely captivated him to
hear a girl say she could scorn an offer of marriage from
him.

"The golden-haired daughter of the Colonel, to whose
pure mind affectation and insincerity were unknown ideas,
and in whose thoughts always lingered a dim remem·
brance of waving forests and wigwam fires, simply laid
her hand in the Lieutenant's and accepted him without
asking for 'time to think it over on account of its being
so sudden and unexpected.'

"A double wedding soon took place, with all the elegance the Fort could command, and the Colonel and his
wife were congratulated on all sides upon the success of
their beautiful daughters. And the sisters by adoption
became sisters-in-law, but none the less continued to love
each other devotedly.

"Their little infant daughters, who came to brighten
the regiment, one cold, snowy Christmas season, were
each, of course, duly christened Kiamush, and the gold
beads were put upon one, and the little coral necklace
upon the other.

"In due time they entered Vassar and graduated with
honor, and there were no two more brilliant girls in **my**
class than they.

"What career lies before them in the future has not as yet been determined."

"And now we'll hear from Princeton," said the Colonel, decisively, with a Jove-like nod of his head towards the Senior Captain. "Collegians are scarce in this crowd——"

"You forget Vassar, Colonel," promptly interposed Mr. Briggs, with a glance that plainly intimated that he had not forgotten Dot.

"I beg a thousand pardons—I should have said 'among the men.' I meant it. Come, Captain, it is your turn," and a murmur of approbation followed as once more he turned to his staunch supporter—the right of his line in more ways than one.

The Senior Captain twisted his moustache thoughtfully, and began :

THE SENIOR CAPTAIN'S STORY.

"I once attended a Christmas surprise party to which I wasn't invited. If you'll pass the Maraschino I'll tell you about it, for it really was no end of fun to me at any rate. It was at Fort Sage. Most of you know the place. It was Christmas-eve, and there had been the usual Christmas trees and small family gatherings at the married officers' quarters, and a rather stiff egg-nogg at the mess. As I passed the quarters of Colonel Hume a cheery light streaming over the spectral snow seemed to hold out an invitation which I did not care to resist. There was something in the old fellow's dry and bitter humor which flavored his conversation. Did you harbor any illusions or cherish any ideals, he would dispel the one and dethrone the other with a cheerful alacrity which reminded one of the merry hangman in 'Quentin Durward.' Consequently he was much sought by the youngsters whose hearts had been shriveled in passing through the Sahara of West Point. The door was opened by Mrs. Lynch, relict of musician Michael Lynch, who in life had tortured the trombone. Round and comfortable as to figure, with the frosty bloom of a winter apple, she smiled indulgently upon me.

" ' Is the Colonel in yet, Mrs. Lynch?' I asked.

" ' Indade he's not, sor, and it's no sayin' whin he'll be ; but come in and kape out of the cold, sor; ye know where ye'll find the pipes and the 'baccy.'

" I followed her into the Colonel's cosy den, which he dignified by the name of library, and lighting a favorite Powhatan, with a long cane stem, I sank into a deep arm-chair and resigned myself to sensuous content made up of warmth, tobacco. and eggnogg. I was roused from a delightful lethargy by the Colonel stamping the snow off his boots. As he came in, his jolly red face glowing, in his big buffalo coat, was the picture of good humor ; but a second glance showed the hard lines which trouble had graven deeply around his mouth.

'In the gloaming, oh, my darling,' chirped the old gentleman. 'Musing over the coals like a true-hearted bachelor, for which nature cut you out, my boy ; but like many other duffers you knew better than the old lady, and behold the result. You forsake the fatted calf to browse on the husks, and that on Christmas-eve. Come, now'—drawing up a chair beside me, and filling his pipe—' tell the honest truth ; isn't there a flavor about the husks which you don't get in the domestic veal? Marriage, my boy, is a bit of music with lots of variations, but somehow or other you can't arrange them so that the discords will not be heard. Gad, in old times they used to make hermits out of scamps ; we've improved on that, we reform them by turning them into husbands. I haven't a word to say against love ; it may be silly, but it isn't incurable. Beside, love's a necessary evil ; it was nature's first production, and she ought to have stopped then; but, like a great many other successful authors, she must try a sequel. She got too many properties on her stage ; tried to make a spectacular drama out of a two-character piece written in the only language which survived the Tower of Babel, with no scenery but the grass under foot and the trees overhead. I liked the original, but didn't care for the sequel. Too much style and gew-gaws.

> " ' Marian's married and I sit here
> Alone and merry at forty year,
> Dipping my nose in the Gascon wine '—

" ' Speaking of wine, will you have a drink ? '

" ' Thanks, none for me,' I replied. ' The egg-nogg was decidedly potent.'

" Silence fell upon us both and the Colonel seemed to be seeking the dead past in the rapidly-fading embers.

" ' So you did have a Marian,' I ventured, feeling an uncontrollable desire to drop a tentative lead into the unexplored depths of the Colonel's past.

" ' Yes,' replied the Colonel. And a still longer silence followed.

" ' I believed it all as fondly, as blindly, as besottedly, as the poor dupe who went to sleep a caliph and woke up a pauper. One day my happiness turned all I touched, even the commonest things, to gold : the next the heart I believed priceless proved, at the sight and touch of gold, base metal. I beg her pardon ; she was simply a dutiful daughter. Her parents said, "My child, a rich man wishes to marry you ; throw that heart away and be a woman." Of course she obeyed them ; that's all there was of it. But what's the use of abusing women ; I haven't found men so much better. Did you know that I had a nephew of whom I grew as fond as I think one man can well be of another. I began to feel that fate had made me some amends in giving me sympathy and good fellowship in exchange for a dream.'

"Here the Colonel stopped. I rather indicated than spoke a single word. 'Dead ?'

"'No, worse ; a blackguard, whether alive or dead, I don't know. I did all I could, but he was bound to go to the bad. The last thing I heard of him he had married a pretty girl to spoil her life I suppose. What an infernal muddle it all is.'

"The door slyly opened and the rubicund countenance of Mrs. Lynch diffused a mellow radiance. 'Kurnel, I'm axin' yer pardon for presuming to inthrude, but the good ladies have sint you an ilegant Christmas gift what'll kape you warrm this bitter cold night and they laid a promise on me that I'd show it you before ye wint to bed.'

"'Christmas Carols and coals of fire all in a lump,' I cried ; 'you undeserving sinner, you've been abusing your best friends.'

"'Come along,' he replied, 'let's see what it's like. If it's anything to warm the inner man we'll take a nip.'

"Mrs. Lynch led the way with conscious pride into a cheerful room with a clear fire glowing in the grate and brightly lighted by several wax candles in old-fashioned silver candlesticks evidently to do honor to the gift. There it was, laid across the bed – a rich, bright-colored silk quilted coverlid, and slightly moving in the centre was something white, which, as we drew near in speechless surprise, revealed a veritable snow-flake, which might have drifted on the winter wind from some far-off fairy land. A closer inspection showed that the snow-flake had a chubby fist crammed into its mouth and was winking contentedly at the firelight, as the Colonel and I stared helplessly from the apparition to one another.

"Mrs. Lynch whispered, 'Holy Mother of God! it's an angel came to us this blessed Christmas eve.' At this critical moment, as if to disclaim such lofty origin, the fist was slowly withdrawn, the eyes disappeared into innumerable puckers and the snow-flake was merged into a mouth which emitted a yell out of all proportion to its size. Mrs. Lynch made a dash for the recreant cherub, but the Colonel seized her roughly by the arm.

"'Stuff and nonsense! some trick,' said he. 'Bridget, have you a hand in this; did you let that thing in the house? Take it away this instant.'

"'Indade and it's God's truth I'm tellin' you,' she panted, trying to quiet the vociferous infant. 'When I left the room to call you there was not a livin' thing in it savin' the quilt, which I put on the bed wid me own hands; sorra's the day that I'd be bringin' throuble on you, sor, and all that ye've done for me and mine.'

"'Take it away,' the Colonel repeated helplessly.

"The little fellow, attracted by the buttons, for the Colonel had donned his best blouse in honor of the evening's festivities, stretched out his chubby little hands with a gurgle of delight. The Colonel's face softened. It wasn't in human nature, certainly not in his, to be proof against that base infantile stratagem. 'I suppose they trained you to do that, you little beggar, before they sent you out to impose upon people—here, take it away.'

7

"'Where shall I take it, sor?' whimpered Mrs. Bridget.

"'Anywhere, anywhere! Give it to the Captain here'; let him take it home to his wife.'

"'You are very generous, but I could not think of depriving you of such a priceless treasure,' said I. 'Now if you were to offer me the quilt I might be induced to accept.'

"You be d—d,' he retorted, with such hearty emphasis that I realized that any more teasing would imperil the chances of the poor little waif, of whom I had already become a warm partisan.

"Bridget had, in the mean time, drawn a chair to the fire and, with her new-found treasure in her lap, was rubbing and warming his little feet. She looked up anxiously at the Colonel's explosion. 'Only mind the little darlin' stretchin' his toes to the fire; shure, sor, you will kape the poor lamb this night. It wud be bad luck, to say nothin' of ingratitude to the blessed Christ, to turn one of His little ones away, and it the holy Christmas eve.'

"'What the devil can I do else?' snapped the Colonel. 'Can I put five cents in his hand and tell him to go to the next house? Here, put him to bed and see that he doesn't howl.'

"'Howl, is it? I am only hopin' ye may have as swate a slape. My respects to ye both, gintlemin, and wishin' you a Merry Christmas, and ye'll desarve it, Kurnel, barrin' your talkin' of sendin' the crayture away, and ye'd not turn out a starvin' dog,' and the good woman disappeared with a suspicious moisture in her eyes.

"The spectacle of utter content exhibited by the dire disturber of our peace as he triumphantly rode off on Mrs. Lynch's shoulder was too much for even the Colonel's worriment, and we both laughed heartily; but with the closing door he turned to me with an expression of hopeless perplexity. 'Nice situation, upon my soul! When you see the Quartermaster to-morrow, my boy, ask him if he will have a sign painted for my front door, *Foundling Asylum!* I might as well face the music; by this time to-morrow the old post gossips will have got the yarn in embellished form.'

"'Colonel,' said I, 'what is your idea about this? You do not suspect a trick, do you?'

"'No,' he said, emphatically; 'not in the way of a joke. We have our fair allowance of fools, but I think not any absolute curs; beside, what woman would lend a child for such a purpose? There is no hope of any such solution. Some one was watching Mrs. Lynch through the window and slipped in as soon as she left the room. You see it opens into that short passage with a door leading to the garden. I am afraid it is a Bootles' baby business, and yet I do not think I have made any enemy sufficiently clever to devise such a revenge.'

"'More likely,' I said, 'that some one, knowing that you have a woman's heart under your bear's hide, has simply put on you the onus of turning out a child that they were unable or unwilling to provide for.'

"'Yes, possibly some poor devil on the verge of starvation. Well! I suppose I must keep it until I find its owner.'

"'Good-night, old man,' I replied. 'I wish you success in your new *rôle*—Japhet in search of a father or mother, you are not particular which. At any rate you have a new interest in life, and I am almost tempted to hope that the mystery may never be cleared up. It would be so delightful to see your acceptance of the duties and responsibilities of matrimony. You are atoning nobly

for the crime of abusing it. Good-night, papa! good-
night and a Merry Christmas to the whole family. I'll
look in to-morrow morning.'   Then I left abruptly, for.
there were fire-shovels, canes, pokers and umbrellas un-
pleasantly handy for missile weapons.

"Christmas morning came cold and clear, as it only
comes on the great plains ; so still that nature seemed to
have stopped breathing.   Smoke floated up in a tall, ver-
tical column till it blended with the clear blue, and the
monotonous outlines of a woodless country assumed purity
and beauty veiled in maiden white. As one officer after
another emerged, hearty greetings and merry laughter
rang upon the frosty air, the only Christmas bells in that
distant region.   About eleven o'clock I went to Colonel
Hume's quarters.   Mrs. Lynch, rustling in the stiff dignity of her Christmas gown, opened the door and ushered
me at once into the presence of His Majesty, who was en-
throned upon the kitchen table, where he could oversee
his realm, while his obedient hand-maiden cooked the
Colonel's Christmas turkey.   In the corner was a branch
from one of·the few stunted evergreens which grew upon
the reservation, set in a tub of sand and ashes and hung
with gay-colored glass balls and strings of rock candy.
The little fellow was literally smothered in drums and
horses and woolly dogs, from the midst of which he crowed
delightedly.   It was evident that Mrs. Lynch had sacked
the sutler's store at an early hour.   I am almost ashamed
to say how much I was moved at the sight of this little
waif brought in from cold and hunger to the warmth and
welcome of a motherly heart, and I thought : ' Inasmuch
as ye have done it unto one of the least of these." Alas !
the spirit of unrest and grasping ambition had entered
the infantile Paradise.   In one of his frantic grabs at a
woolly dog, with evident intention of sucking the paint

off, he grasped his own toe, and, utterly unmindful of feasible joys, he devoted every faculty to the task of getting it into his mouth, with the result of rolling over, to the injury of the dog, and at imminent risk of falling off the table. A scream, a frantic rush, and the squirming mass of baby and toe was rescued from its perilous position. After duly praising and patting the prodigy I went in search of the Colonel, pondering much over the diamonds in rough of some natures and the delicacy and poetry inherent in the Irish heart.

"As it was about 12 o'clock, I bent my steps to the mess, for I knew that there was high carnival there. As I entered, bursts of laughter punctuated a story which some one was telling. I found all the mess gathered round the Colonel, and I concluded that he had taken the bull by the horns and was telling the story on himself.

"On the table, in the centre of the room, stood a great bowl of steaming apple-toddy of true Virginia make and flavor, for had not one of the longest-legged sons of the old Dominion that ever bestrode a calvary-horse mingled the ingredients with loving care? On a smaller table at one side stood a glass bowl containing an insinuating and deadly punch, the work of a scion of innumerable Knickerbockers, who brought to this far-off wilderness a flavor of Rockaway and Tuxedo, our swell par-excellence Lieutenant Cortlandt, the adjutant of the post. The Colonel nodded pleasantly to me, and went on with his story: 'Where was I? oh, yes, I was just at the climax. The old woman dragged us into the bedroom to see the present ; and what do you suppose we found?' here he made the usual dramatic pause.

"'If the women on the post knew you as well as we do,' drawled Brokenborough, the tall Virginian, in his musical vernacular, 'you found a five-gallon jug of good whiskey.'

"'To tell you the truth,' said the Colonel, 'that was what I rather expected to find, but when we entered the room we were partially blinded by the combined effect of wax candles and the loveliest coverlid you ever laid eyes on.'

"'Kind that you win at a charity bazar and give it b-back to be p-put up next night,' suggested Cortlandt.

"'Nothing of the sort,' said the Colonel; 'something that such a graceless scamp as you need never hope to attain. Well, as soon as our eyes became accustomed to this blaze of glory, we noticed something wiggling in the middle of the coverlid, and as I live it was neither more nor less than a real, live, kicking baby.'

"'Great Scott!' shouted the club in Gilbertian chorus.

"'I pitched into the old woman, and she swore there was nothing on the bed but the quilt when she left the room to call me in and show me the present, and I do believe that to this moment she thinks it came from above. I ordered her to throw it out of the window, but Bridget and my friend, here the Captain, begged so hard for the kid that I consented to give it a night's lodging.'

"'You old dog in the manger,' I retorted, 'you felt that it was nothing on earth but poetic justice overtaking you for the way you've abused men whose happiness you envied, and you took your medicine like a little man.

"'It's well you did, for I've just come from your quarters, and if anybody on this earth can truly sing "I'm monarch of all I survey," it's that identical kid. Bridget has it seated on the kitchen-table, with the whole contents of the sutler's store spread around it, and a brilliantly-decorated Christmas-tree in the ash can in one corner. She stops basting the turkey to kiss the baby, and I am afraid you will have under-done turkey and over-done baby for dinner.

"The club laughed with evident enjoyment of the Colonel's discomfiture.

Brokenborough said, 'If you don't want him, Colonel, you can turn him over to the base-ball club for a mascot.'

'Give him to me,' said Courtland ; 'I'll make a t-tiger of him one of these days.''

"'Gentlemen, said old Paddy Byrne, the jolliest Irishman in the service, 'you're treating this event with undue levity. It's a momentous step in the career of my distinguished friend, and there's fine precedents for it. Didn't the Emperor Napoleon, when he was just as good as a bachelor, adopt Prince Eugene ? I'm sincerely glad that this Maverick has turned up to occupy a corner in the heart that's intirely too large for the proprietor all by himself. May it grow up to be the prop of his declining years. Gentlemen, we drink the health of Colonel Hume and his adopted son.'

"After this the fun became general and the Colonel was given a respite.

"'Come,' he said, taking me by the arm, 'let us go to the house and see if there's any prospect of solving this mystery.'

"When we reached the door, Mrs. Lynch rushed out to meet us. 'Oh, Kurnel!' she fairly screamed, 'I've found her !'

"'The devil you have !' he replied. 'Twin sister, I suppose. With your peculiar talent for finding babies, Bridget, the whole family will be here before morning. The fellow who takes rabbits out of his hat was a duffer to you ; how do you manage it ?'

"'How you will be talkin', sor ; I mane the mother, and a fine, dacint woman she is, and she was starvin', and she could get a place barrin' that she had the baby, and so ——'

"'Well, well, come in and finish your story; it is too cold to be standing outside,' and he led her to the warmth and comfort of the library. 'Now, tell us how you found her, what she has to say for herself, and why she brought it here.'

"'Well, sor, ye know I'd not be likin' to lave it long for fear of its hurtin' itself, but I just stepped across the way to Mrs. Redmond's to borrow from the cook a little spice for me puddin'. Whin I come back, there was this young woman down on her knees sobbin' over the baby and smudderin' it wid kisses, and talkin' wild like, and callin' down all the blessin's of heavin on thim that had tuk pitty on her baby, and threated it like it was their own.'

"'I see it all, Bridget; you need tell me no more. You got up and looked at each other and then fell to hugging the baby.'

"'Not at all, sor; I was for orderin' her out o' the house, but she stud up on her feet and looked me in the face, and there was somethin' about her, sor,—not that she was well dressed, but somethin'—you'll understand, sor, —that told me she had seen better days.'

"'I would like to see her,' said the Colonel. 'Can't you get her to come in and tell me her story?'

"'I'm afraid, sor, that it'll frighten her away, and if she goes off in this bither cold weather, she will be dead before mornin'—she's that wake and miserable.'

"'Bless my soul!' exclaimed the Colonel; 'I must go and see her. Go ahead, Bridget; but I am afraid it is too late; she must have heard us talking.'

"'Niver you mind that, sor. I slipped the key in me pocket, whin I came in the house, and she'll not get out of the window, and she barely able to stand.'

"The Colonel followed Bridget, but as he approached

I heard a faint scream, and a woman dashed past him, evidently making for the front door. Seeing me, she stopped with the helpless look of a hunted animal, her feet seemed to give way, and she fell into the nearest chair and endeavoring to hide her face. The glimpse I had showed a figure tall and well made, but painfully thin. Her face, when she f ally raised it—well, I can't describe a woman, but if any of you have ever seen the Beatrice, —I don't mean the smiling damsel of the copies, who has put on a coquettish turban for a masquerade, but the soul-haunting picture of Guido—that face in which grief has crushed out the beauty—you can fancy what she looked like. The Colonel came in, evidently at his wits' end, but when he saw that face the grand old fellow showed of what stuff he was made. I wish some of the women who think him only a bear could have seen him. He spoke to her as gently as if she had been his own daughter, come home after long and weary wanderings ; and as she looked up at him, she seemed to read the true goodness and tenderness of his heart, for she made an effort to rise and speak. But he laid a kind hand upon her, saying, 'Why do you wish to run away from us? We are your friends here. Come, tell me all about yourself, and how you came to be in such trouble. Bridget bring a glass of wine and biscuit,' and wheeling her chair up to the fire, he made her drink the wine ; then placing himself beside her, he waited patiently till she had strength to speak.

" 'Oh, sir,' she said, raising her tearful eyes to him, 'what can I say, to thank you and bless you for your goodness ? I had only meant to steal in and give my poor baby one last kiss ; but the sight of his happiness, and all that this good woman had done for him, overcame me entirely, for, as you see, I am not very strong.

7*

" ' I had lost my husband, I was without a cent, and I could get no work, burdened with the young child. No one wants a woman with a baby. In my distress, not knowing where to turn, I remembered my mother's words : ' If you ever need a friend go to Colonel Hume, tell him frankly whose daughter you are, and though I wronged him bitterly, he loved me as only such men can love, and will cherish no unkindness to the dead.'

" ' Then you are poor Mary's daughter.' The old Colonel's lip trembled, and he took the poor, thin hand in his and lifted it reverentially to his lips. ' My dear,' he said, ' I never loved but one woman, and her daughter cannot want a home or friend while I live—and who was your husband ? '

" ' I married against my parents' will, and a short time after my father had money troubles, his health gave way, he died and we were left penniless. My mother did not long survive him, and after her death my husband was more and more unfortunate, and in his misery he sought the worst of all consolations ; one thing after another was sold or pawned, until nothing was left. He finally enlisted, and died soon after he got to this post. I have some skill as an artist, and managed to get together enough to come to him when I heard of his illness. He died before I reached here. The rest you know. Can you forgive the mad step I took, and think of me as a woman who had but one ray of hope on earth and blindly followed it ? '

" ' Your husband enlisted as a private in the —th ; and what was his name ? ' asked the Colonel.

" She answered, with evident reluctance : ' Arthur Hume.'

" ' Great Heavens ! my unfortunate nephew ! '

" ' I know how badly you thought of him,' she pleaded,

'but indeed he was never unkind to me when he was sober.'

"Poor girl, what a pitiful revelation lay beneath those words!

"'I'll say nothing hard of him now,' said the Colonel gently, 'but I will hope, Marie, that your boy may fill in both of our hearts the place of those we have loved and lost.'

"At this moment Mrs. Lynch re-entered, bearing the baby in her arms. Marie rose and clasped him tightly to her breast.

"'Never more to part, dear little one,' she said; 'we have found some one to love us.'

"'Yes, my dear niece,' replied the Colonel, 'this must be your home always.'

"'Oh, uncle, that would be too much of a burden for you, a baby in the house. We will live near you, and I can work.'

"'No, no, my dear,' said Colonel Hume, stroking the baby's cheek; 'you gave him to me and you cannot take him back. This little child has brought again to me the happy days of youth and love. He has found his way to my old heart, and it shall be his as long as I live. Captain, bring your good wife over this evening, and we will have a happy Christmas, and you shall see how diligently the old bachelor will make up for all the years of happiness he has lost.'"

And then, with the "sma' hours" beginning to grow anything but wee, the tireless party turned on the soldier who sat at the place of honor at the right of the Colonel's wife. No one could think of going home without a story from his lips. He had told not a few, but each was fresh, new, quainter even than its predecessor, full of the oddest, brightest thoughts and similes, bubbling over with a humor inexhaustible as the famous spring of Rhenish Prussia, and to the full as cool and sparkling. It was useless for him to beg off. He might have known they would not go without

THE COLONEL'S STORY; OR, ORRIKER'S EARRINGS.

"Probably none of you ever met Lieutenant Orriker? I believe he was before your time."

"Never heard of him, Colonel."

This was said by the Assistant Post-Surgeon, in whose direction the Colonel happened to be looking. Then recollecting he was in his first year of service, the Assistant blushed violently and resolved he would not be betrayed into another word no matter what turned up.

"Well, Orriker resigned years ago. He was an old crony of mine, and what I am going to tell you is a bit of genuine history."

Between ourselves, the incident was entirely of home production, but a modest man talks more freely about his neighbors than himself, so the Colonel took refuge behind a personality only to be found in very old army recollections.

Just here, however, the Colonel's wife, who wore a light scarf upon her shoulders, folded this rather hastily over her head, and the Quartermaster, who knew something of drafts, got up and closed the door behind the madam, for which he was rewarded with a smile that had in it, he thought, as much amusement as thanks. And the Assistant-Surgeon looked grimly on and said to himself, "Ah, ha! she is a bit of a coquette still."

This little confusion over, the Colonel began:

"It certainly was a singular ornament that attracted

the attention of Lieutenant Orriker as he passed the window—only a pair of earrings—but of such a curious make that another look was inevitable, and then another, until the conviction arose that those earrings were of no common origin or associations.

"The pen that Tennyson uses, or the telescope that Wellington held, may readily be supposed to acquire some subtile atmosphere of their own that could strengthen the poet's or the soldier's eye and help him to visions and combinations beyond ordinary reach ; nor was the savage altogether wrong who desired to dine on his rival's heart in order that he might secure some portion of his rival's courage.

"So in the sparkle of these earrings the Lieutenant seemed to see, as in a magic glass, the graceful forms and draperies of foreign lands moving to strange melodies, and even to him out there on the street came a faint fragrance of incense and spices that belonged rather to Arabian than New England nights.

"In his walk the next morning he suddenly found himself looking into the window as before, but the earrings were gone, and he began to realize what an impression they had made, and how much he wanted them.

"For he had found out that a certain birthday was not far off which called for agreeable notice, and where selection was difficult it was wise to begin early.

"Nothing declared itself that had a tithe of the fascination of those earrings, and apparently he had lost them by his delay.

"A day or two passed, and again the Lieutenant stood at the window, and there they were in the corner, half covered by newer and far more conventional jewelry. The opportunity, so strangely recovered, as the Lieutenant thought, was not to be resisted, and they were secured, notwithstanding what looked like reluctance on the part of the salesman to let them go.

"The conversation brought out a fear that they would not be likely to suit, 'they were very old-fashioned,' etc., etc., and the inference was permitted that they were no part of the stock imported from the metropolis to do credit to modern taste, but a parcel left for disposal that had become necessary, rather than coveted.

"Truly they resembled all choice works of nature or of art in that the longer you looked at them the larger they grew, reaching out into the unlimited and ineffable, as if the matter ordinarily there was only a part of finer existences, ever declaring themselves in wholes more and more complete.

"We have been told, on very good authority, to go to the ant, learn of her and be wise, wisdom evidently pertaining to the female in case of this particular insect. But the ant lays up a good deal she does not need, and men are just as foolish.

"The earrings had been gained, the birthday came, but love's young dream had dissolved and left no use for the trinket, which catastrophe belongeth not to this story.

"Suffice it to say that the earrings were temporarily loaned to a sympathizing cousin, who was to take care of them till wanted, if, in the future, another vision should materialize and remain constant long enough for a birthday to put in an appearance."

Here the Colonel's wife filled up his glass as a delicate intimation that he was getting too morose for a mixed audience.

"Thank you, my dear," said the Colonel; "I was a little melancholy, thinking of poor Orriker." Then the Colonel went on: "Coming home from church one day, Cousin Cornelia, to her horror, discovered that one earring was missing. Oh, it was in the bonnet—it may be on the table—it might have been dropped in the hall—it could have fallen by the steps—it must be in the pew—certainly.

"But the search, notwithstanding its thoroughness deserved success, was unavailing, which was quite vexatious, for Cousin Orriker really seemed in a fair way to find further use for his investment.

"When told of the loss, he determined to recover the earring, being one of those men who only get interested in impossibilities, he hunted sidewalk, street and aisle, the search becoming occupation for any odd moment left over from guard-mounting and drill, which, in those days, as later, formed the whole duty of the subaltern.

"But the earring remained a mystery, like the tomb of Moses, till some time afterwards the Lieutenant found himself on the ferry-boat, thinking of the Seminole war and looking at a lady. Although she was not exactly opposite him, yet his eye traveled back to her with a pertinacity that was annoying, and not to be accounted for by anything peculiar in ribbons or complexion, when at last he actually caught a glimpse of the earring upon her bosom.

"It was a delicate matter to pursue, and he was reduced to such investigation as he could make in a tour of the cabin, up and down, with his discovery as the objective-point.

"Sure enough, there it was,—a gold sphere, swinging in a crescent, with a tiny gold star as pendant, and the curious inlaid arabesque along both crescent and sphere, dotted with ruby and diamond-dust.

"But it was mounted as the head of a shawl-pin, and that, apparently, was its original shape.

"Orriker determined to locate the bearer, but she went to the railway-rooms and passed the gate at once to the cars.

"The Lieutenant gallantly cut his military duties for that afternoon, bought a ticket, as soon as he could, for the nearest outside station on a venture. He was barely in time for a train which he searched closely without flushing his game, and upon inquiry learned that an 'express' preceded the 'local' by a minute or so, making its first stop too far out to admit of further pursuit.

"He had the pleasure of a wait-over at East Essex three hours or so for the down train, and did not improve the opportunity by any exhaustive study of the advertisement-boards, like the traveler way-bound at Didcot Junction, who, it will be remembered, became so interested in the etymological possibilities of Edward Chapman Allington, and developed therefrom a long chronicle of English history, as my audience under like circumstances are earnestly advised to do.

"The Lieutenant had some trouble in making his peace with the post commander, to whom he had been reported absent, and who, he felt, was too old a soldier to take any stock in argonaut expeditions in these days of schedules and clocks and subsidy steamers. He concluded to take the matter up logically. His adventure began with the .1 P.M. ferry-boat. The lady evidently was traveling on a season ticket; a reason for taking the 2 P.M. train on one Wednesday might hold good for another. He would be on hand accordingly.

"So he was often, and with no reward. Looking up, however, from a brown study at a sudden stop of the street-car one morning, there, right beside him, he saw again the sparkle of the earring.

"At least so it seemed. Sphere, crescent, star, scroll and all were visible enough, but unfortunately on the bosom of a very different woman. He had made no cata-logue of the features of the first, but certainly she was a Saxon, while his present neighbor as certainly belonged to the order of the olive. It seemed useless to follow up the clue. There must be many individual ornaments of the same type and he had the proof of it before him.

"So the Lieutenant took himself to the oldest jewelry establishment within his reach, left the odd earring to be made into a charm for his watch-chain and encouraged conversation on the subject. Mr. Goldsmith examined the specimen closely and became very much interested in it, pronounced it unique and said nothing of the sort had been on the market within his recollection ; that, in fact, it was totally opposed to current styles and properly be-longed, not to a modern ear, but to the —— Museum.

"In this conclusion the Lieutenant recognized the trade-mark and resolved to get back his earring if it took him to Africa. He would put the quest on as high a footing as the San Grael itself and prosecute it in single-ness of heart without a thought of tactics, Tampa Bay or trial by court-martial.

"Every Wednesday afternoon found him at the depot with a fixed purpose to follow, though

"' His path was rugged and sore,
Through tangled juniper, beds of reeds,
Through many a fen where the serpent feeds,
And man never trod before.'

"But it was a waste of time. His ticket for East Es-sex, good until used, was as unprofitable an investment as Lamon's 'Life of Lincoln' or the 'Military Encyclo-pedia.'

"It came to pass, however, that the Lieutenant, in walking up Willington Street some days afterwards, met an open gate which he kicked to rather unceremoniously just as an elderly lady appeared on the steps beyond and started down the walk. She seemed quite feeble, and the Lieutenant, afraid that, in his violence, he had thrust the gate over its natural limit, pulled it back again with considerable trouble. He had not, therefore, noticed that meantime she had been joined by a much younger person until, as they passed out together, suddenly the shawl-pin flashed into view in the dress of the latter, but assuredly under a face that he had never yet seen.

"Now some faces grow upon you like the contents of a walnut, which are the reward only of the most searching examination. And some faces show all they have at once, like a bunch of grapes, and some resemble persimmons, that are never sweet until after a touch of frost, and give as little promise in the beginning of the result as a California nugget offers of one of Cellini's medallions.

"Orriker was getting to be quite a connoisseur in physiognomy, and his interest in the shawl-pin was almost eclipsed by his sudden wonder who could own those eyes,

> "'Darker than the depth
> Of water stilled at even.'

"This appearance, too, of no less than three shawl-pins, all of them composed apparently of the lost ear-ring, could only suggest to the baffled Lieutenant uneasy suspicions of monomania. Was it not really getting to be the case that he was projecting an ideal object of search into an objective existence upon the bosom of every lady that he met?

"Not a little stunned by this last encounter and revolving the problem of entire ownership of his wits, he had gone some distance before he recollected that it might be useful to mark down the locality of this last surprise.

"He turned back and was confronted by a new puzzle. There were no less than three houses all with like fronts, like paths and like gates on the same side of the street, and Lieutenant Orriker, more than ever convinced that for him all roads were leading to Bloomingdale, went home to get among friends and prepare for the worst.

"By a night's sleep he was greatly refreshed and a thorough wigging he received from his captain for failure to sign up the clothing-book gave him much comfort. He was enabled to orient himself and get a sure hold upon his identity.

"He proceeded to distribute a score or so of autographs over the company records with as much self-reliance as 'Charles Carroll of Carrollton' felt when he signed an earlier and quite as valuable a document. Satisfied then that life was not an illusion nor his sanity a dream in spite of the three shawl-pins, he went into the necessary inquiries as to the occupants of Willington Street, but only to be persuaded that the two ladies he had met bore no relation to any of the houses in question except that of visitors.

"Nothing that answered his description of the pair could be developed as properly belonging to that neighborhood. Perhaps he was too oblivious of the fact that beauty, like the prophets, is without honor in its own country, and that everybody makes for himself his rainbows, and *beaux yeux* as well.

"But during the campaign he one day stepped into the local Dorlan's to get something to eat. Looking about in the unpleasant quarter-of-an-hour that preludes the composition of your order, he suddenly lost all appetite in the endeavor to comprehend that but a few feet from him

were seated all three of the Graces. The longer he looked
the more certain he was, not only of the passenger on the
ferry-boat, but also of his neighbor in the street-car, and,
above all, the angel by the gate.

" Here they were seated at the same table, finishing their
lunch, but apparently in no hurry. Devoutly did the
Lieutenant pray for haste in his own case, and delay in
theirs, like the parishioners on opposite sides of the county
who wanted rain and dry weather in the same week.

" Finally they gathered up their gloves and wrappings
and a few minor parcels, and it then became evident that
one thing was lacking—truly the key to the whole position. Nowhere was visible the shawl-pin—not a trace of
it on the person of any of the three.

" Nevertheless, he was sure of the faces, and as they
got up to go, the Lieutenant bolted from the premises and
awaited them at the curb.

" Just then the waiter appeared with an anxious face,
somewhat relieved at sight of his customer, who was doing considerable thinking to the minute.

" His first impulse was to toss the boy a dollar under
plea of a forgotten engagement. But in that view of the
case it was impossible to wait upon the convenience of the
ladies, who were leisurely talking to one another, as those
who had the whole day before them.

" Orriker nodded to John, and said : ' All right, I'll be
there in a moment ;' but John seemed suspicious, and
remained on guard ready for emergencies. The situation
was getting to be noticeable and had to be terminated.
Clearly he had no warrant for introducing himself.
American etiquette, though without its Brummell or
court-guide, does not permit a gentleman to accost a
group of girls, simply because of

" ' Eyes that do mislead the morn,'

or inferences based upon the supposed possession of curious jewelry.

"The ladies passed out of sight round the corner, and the Lieutenant went back to his chops and tomato sauce.

"Making his way to the table previously occupied by the three fair strangers, and, astonished to find that instead of marble, it was the plainest of pine, now they had gone, he saw on one of the chairs a small parcel, which he picked up and again rushed to the street, while the waiter, turning in time to see this second hegira, followed him with a frantic 'Hold on, there!' that brought matters to a crisis.

"To make a first appearance in the highest circles of society as a fugitive from culinary complications, enforced by an irate youth in a white apron, was not to be endured.

"The Lieutenant pocketed for the present both parcel and affront, brought back to his lunch the absent air of a man much pre-occupied by business engagements, hung up his hat with great deliberation and enlarged his order to include a dessert and a pint of champagne, in order that the establishment might be properly impressed with the ways usual to him when he had time to spare.

"In fact he devoted the next hour in toying with his meat and sipping the cider. Then he handed the waiter a three-dollar bill, ignored the change as proof that he owned more money than he knew what to do with, and departed, having only succeeded in convincing the proprietor of this particular resort that he was a man to be kept under the closest observation hereafter.

"Meanwhile the ladies had resumed their shopping. As a matter of course, a soda-water fountain came in their way, and there being an hour still to wait, they decided to spend it in a photograph-gallery, so reaching the railroad-station just in time for the 4 o'clock express.

"But now the loss of the parcel was first discovered, with mutual exclamations of surprise and alarm. Each was sure the other had it, and there was the familiar search of pockets and reticules. 'Oh! here it is!—no—I remember now—this is it—where can it be?'

"Train or parcel, which? The result was, apparently, a change of programme—Miss Louise to go to the gallery, Miss Mary to the soda-water man, and Miss Jane to the store, all to meet at the lunch-rooms, as they all duly did, with no success.

"After a brief discussion the proprietor and his assistant, recollecting all that happened, declared their belief that the young fellow with the three-dollar bill and the new moustache was responsible for the trouble, on the satisfactory ground that if two odd things occur in the course of an hour, one must be the cause of the other.

"Now follows a strange thing. Lieutenant Orriker had been looking for an earring, and in a few days had found at least three; but here were six people hunting one another: the waiter and Dorlon after the young fellow with the new moustache; the ladies carefully scrutinizing every wearer of that appendage, and Orriker himself patiently devoting his leisure to the pursuit of the pretty girl with the blue eyes, the beautiful girl with the black eyes and that rare epitome of everything lovely, with eyes that beggared Solomon's Song, deeper than the speculations of Plato, darker than the iambics of Lycophron, sweeter than the strains of the great god Pan, when

> "'The sun on the hill forgot to die
> And the lilies revived, and the dragon-fly
> Came back to dream on the river,'

and all in vain.

"The Lieutenant had visited the railway station,

coming, of course, by one door as the girls left by the other. Soda water and photographs were peculiarities of feminine interest that had so far escaped his analysis, and as for the lunch-rooms, he was creditably fighting the doubt whether he could ever redeem his self-respect without cuffing that waiter into some appreciation of what a United States Army officer really was.

"But the astonishment of the Lieutenant may be imagined when, on opening the parcel, he found—the shawl-pin itself!

"It was, in every particular, the duplicate of the ear-ring now swinging upon his watch-chain, and had evidently been modified from its original purpose to use as a pin, with slight additions, that had recently undergone repair.

"The box into which it had been put bore no name, nor was there any trace of ownership upon the wrapper save a delicate reminiscence of wild-flowers that subsequently became very familiar to Lieutenant Orriker."

It was at this stage of the story that the Adjutant winked at the Quartermaster's wife, who filliped back a crumb of bread with such accuracy that it knocked off the Assistant-Surgeon's eye-glasses, which he duly remembered in the very next prescription he compounded for that persistent invalid.

"The discussion over the loss of the parcel," continued the Colonel, "grew very interesting. Miss Mary was confident she had left it on the soda-water counter. Miss Louise recollected seeing it at the photograph gallery, and Miss Jane knew for a certainty that it was at one time lying by a box of ribbons on the end desk of the store. In fact, Miss Jane as often as once a week thereafter made sly visits to the suspected spot, and glared suspiciously at the pale maiden with tan-colored braids who was in charge, but no scarf-pin ever came into view.

"It might be as well to state that Miss Jane lived in town. Miss Louise resided some distance out on the Manchester and Essex Railroad, at Palafox Park, while Miss Mary belonged to our side of the Potomac, but was visiting now with one and now with another cousin, including Miss Jane and Louise, and I don't know how many more, for if, with the limited facilities afforded by devotion to business in the North, a Tremont Street man might walk from Boston to Sacramento without finding a relative on the road, a Roanoaker, as the result of the leisure and mint-juleps of the Old Dominion, could take a trip to the Gulf and claim kin on every plantation he crossed.

"Sure enough, Lieutenant Orriker had found the earring, but no peace of mind came with it. What is sought for ceases to please when secured. But it was those wonderful eyes that turned night into day and made a harvest moon as dull as a Sunday-school library or an afternoon in Alexandria.

"It so happened that shortly after these events an invitation from an adjoining town was extended to the troops at the station of the Lieutenant, to participate in the ceremonies of Inauguration Day, and he himself was included in the detail assigned to this amusement.

"Beside the ride, it involved some marching and a dinner, as well as opportunity for a ball that was an irregular appendix to the main affair, out of deference to the instincts of the rural elector, who drew the line at quadrilles and the waltz, of which he knew little, so as to include negro minstrels, and an occasional circus, where he felt more at home.

"No wine was on the table—another evidence of the brotherly consideration that regulates the general appetite by individual prejudice, or, in view of the 'moral vote,' sips its champagne in the closet and shuts off the beer on the street.

"Under these circumstances, the inauguration festivities were not especially attractive to the military mind, but were patiently gone through with, like official boards and tooth-pulling, as part of the discipline of life.

"The chairman of the committee in charge of this particular celebration was, however, something of a soldier himself. His grandfather had served in the old French war, and the present Major Moody felt the drum and fife throbbing in his own blood, and practiced the manual of arms up in the ancestral garret, as laid down in the tactics of 1812–15, having first carefully locked the door to prevent any intrusion upon this unhallowed sport.

"He was determined that the army folks who stayed to dinner should understand that he had outgrown local superstitions, and was posted upon all professional amenities; so, at the close of the parade, he touched the officers upon the shoulder and invited them 'up-stairs.'

"One or two more of the chief people, perhaps the most bewilderingly solemn of all that solemn throng, fell out and followed after, and Orriker was rather appalled, expecting to encounter nothing but a corpse somewhere aloft, for there was a tedious journey down one hallway and up another, past this corner and that, until they all filed into a spare room in the back attic, and Major Moody reverently lifted a napkin and disclosed half a dozen glasses and three decanters of whisky, brandy and Madeira.

"'I know something about campaigning,' said the Major, 'and what soldiers want; just step up, gentlemen, and help yourselves—oh, excuse me, Captain, Lieutenant, this is Squire Sanders, one of our old townsmen, and this is neighbor Pulsifer; now, what will you take?'

8

" ' Thank you, Major,' replied Captain Gilson; ' I am sorry you should have taken all this trouble; I never drink anything, but I shall avail myself of your hospitality to-day—the wine, if you please—Mr. Orriker, let me help you—Mr. Clute, let me fill your glass.'

" Now this was a bold stroke on the part of the Captain, who knew that neither of his Lieutenants, if left to themselves, would take a drop; but he was determined so great an effort to gratify the supposed tastes of strangers in a strange land should not be wholly unrewarded.

" ' Come, squire, come neighbor Pulsifer, you will join us.'

" ' Why, Moody, ah, I should prefer a little of the brandy, but——'

" ' We will both take brandy,' interrupted Captain Gilson, gallantly coming to the rescue and anxious the old gentleman should make the most of so rare a chance, ' allow me the pleasure,' and four tumblers were filled with three good fingers of something that had been in the Major's cellar from before the time of Jefferson's embargo——"

" About 1807," murmured the Assistant-Surgeon to himself; " how nice it would be now——"

" Good, Doctor; I'm thirsty, too," replied the Colonel, and, in due time, continued—

" Well—on the return of the Heraclidæ, that is, when Orriker went down-stairs, right in the parlor doorway he met the girl that had only blue eyes, beautiful, of course, and easier identified as Miss Jane.

" He was in his uniform, which would have prevented any recognition by her; but there were other difficulties. That short mustache which so impressed the waiter, and by which he was handed down in chop-house annals, had been sacrified to a communication from the Post Adjutant,

calling his attention to the predecessor of paragraph
1662, A. R., and the Lieutenant's face was as smooth as
Pope's poetry.

"'May I speak to you one moment?' said he, with the
most academic of bows to Miss Jane; 'I cannot be mistaken, I think; I saw you in company with two ladies at
Mr. Pattycake's some time ago. You left there a small
parcel, which I found and tried to return, but was unable
to discover you.'

"'I believe we left a parcel at Mr. Draper's,' said Miss
Jane, gracious, but positive, and by no means averse to a
discussion of the question with a young man who wore a
uniform as though he had never worn anything else.

"'Possibly, but I found it at the lunch-rooms, a shawl-
pin.'

"'Oh! I am so glad; we were afraid it was lost.'

"'If you will be kind enough to give me your address
I will see to its return—I am very sorry I cannot stay;
my company leaves on the first train——'

"'And the ball?'

"'Oh! that's for Captain Gilson and Mr. Clute; they
remain.'

"'How disagreeable—for you.'

"'Never regretted anything more.'

"But the Lieutenant went home content. Miss Jane
had told him the shawl-pin was Miss Mary's. It could
be left either in town, at 96 Willington Street, or at Palafox Park, where Miss Louise and Miss Mary were staying. In fact, they were all to be together there the next
week, and would be glad to see Mr. Orriker should his
duties leave him time, as was hardly to be supposed.

"Mr. Orriker was very decidedly of the opinion that
with Palafox Park in prospect, his duties would have to
take care of themselves, and so stated, with an emphasis

that had not been so very visible where Willington Street was concerned.

"It might be as well to note that Miss Jane had views on art that were incompatible with anything more than toleration of young men, except so far as a uniform brightened up the landscape and afforded material for effective studies of color.

"Miss Louise was fond of experimenting with every variety of the animal, just as Majendie likes to devote his leisure to rabbits, and Miss Mary had serious ideas of life and doubted the advisability of marriage with anybody under a bishop.

"The prospect for Orriker is by no means so roseate as he thinks.

"However, he appeared at the Park Monday morning, as there was no Sunday train, and Saturday afternoon seemed a little premature."

*   *   *   *   *   *   *   *   *   *

The Colonel shoved his chair back from the table. There was a general burst of expostulation, to which that worthy officer listened with an air of placid surprise, but insisted that he had taken the story to the limits of his own knowledge, and that he was opposed to historical fiction, or mixed aliment of all sorts.

"Why, Colonel," observed the Major, "you remind me of the last war."

"Well, Major, you are always logical, even in your reminiscences ; please explain."

"You started out on a question of search, and you retire without any settlement of the issue."

"Ladies and gentlemen," replied the Colonel, "I refer everybody to my wife. She knows the sequel better than I do. I cannot express to you how flattered I am at the interest you apparently feel in Orriker's earrings. I am going into the library to smoke. Those of you who prefer cigars can join me. Those who prefer the story will of course remain.''

Now this was cruel, but for the credit of the regiment we are glad to be able to say that the Colonel found the library by no means crowded. Not a man budged except the Adjutant, who knew something about the brand of cigar the Colonel used, and would not have postponed the chance of one for Scheherazade herself.

The madam conceded the Adjutant to the pecularities of his taste and station, and, compelled by the presence of the rest, took up the story :

'' These cousins were all well known to me, and it may relieve your curiosity if I say that Miss Jane abandoned art, at the invitation of a professor of mathematics, who married her, and died after working out the properties of a newly-discovered curve, in an equation eight hundred pages long.

'' She subsequently became the wife of a celebrated authority in social statistics, and is now the author of probably the best cook-book written, since it deals with exact quantities, complete rules and ordinary material.

'' Miss Louise married a lieutenant in the navy, with a view of having some time to herself while he was occasionally earning his three years' sea-pay, and as for Miss Mary—her bishop remained behind the ivory gate.''

'' *In partibus infidelium*,'' murmured the Doctor. But the madam thought he was dreaming about some prescription, and so left him to his scruples and drams.

'' Nevertheless,'' said she, '' Lieutenant Orriker had a very pleasant visit at Palafox Park, judging from the number of times it was repeated.

'' The puzzling manifestations of the lost earring were easily explained, inasmuch as when extended into a shawl-pin it became the common property of the three cousins, by whom it was regarded as what is now called a *mascot*, owing to the mystery attending its first appearance.

"It was found one morning at the foot of the stairway, near the shawl-rack and umbrella-stand.

"Nobody knew anything about it and nothing could be ascertained, so it was finally thought possible it had been introduced into the house by the ghost of Miss Mary's godmother, who had recently died in a far-away land and who was reputed to have had, at least, two weaknesses, a fondness for Miss Mary, and a craze for collecting *bijouterie*, pure and undefiled, by the methods and tastes of a commercial and manufacturing age, all of whose work, whether belonging to office or ornament, smacks of petroleum.

"It was very unpleasant for Mr. Orriker to shatter any of the romantic ideals of Palafox Park, but he submitted to their investigation the charm he wore upon his watch-chain, and it seemed evident enough that it was the duplicate of the pin and with it had constituted the purchase formerly made by that gentleman.

"Nevertheless Aunt Mary—not the cousin, but a namesake of an older generation—always affirmed that these same earrings had once belonged to the family, and maintained a silence as to their history that was very provoking, but proof to all solicitation.

"The girls at last admitted that if the dream of the godmother had to be given up, the Lieutenant would not be an altogether unsatisfactory substitute; but he was required to account for the transfer by any less than supernatural means of the earring from the Barracks on the island to Palafox Park.

"The Lieutenant undertook the investigation, but resolved to conduct it after the manner of Penelope, and women generally, who never finish anything in order to always have something to do.

" He very soon satisfied himself that Cousin Jane had on several occasions visited the island where was located the Church of St. Thomas-by-the-sea. This was quite a notorious institution for a variety of reasons. Its rector was young and handsome ; its patrons, wealthy and generous. The harmonies in colored glass that abounded in its walls, the voices of singing men and singing women, that came down from the galleries above, or stole in upon you through the arches and cloisters below, the decorations and the embroidery on the sacred, and the millinery and renown on the profane side of the chancel, made one of the most thoroughly picturesque and attractive interiors to be found in the diocese.

" Perhaps it was not so much a place to tempt a sinful man to pray for mercy as a place of restful repose, where one could recline upon velvet and think of his faith or fortune, just as predominated the wail of a litany or the voluptuous swell of a hallelujah.

"Thus it happened that the aspirations of the artist and the taste of the musician found much satisfaction at Saint Thomas-by-the-sea, and so were brought together Cousin Jane and that Cousin Cornelia of previous mention, wholly unknown to and unconscious of one another then, though one chanced to occupy pew 31, and the other pew 33, on the Easter Sunday of the year to which this story belongs.

" This was a mere matter of dates, which the Lieutenant quietly established, as well as the further fact that Cousin Mary arrived, as arranged, at Palafox Park on the very Sunday night in question, where she was joined by Cousin Jane, and where, the next morning, the earring was found.

"But Mr. Orriker afterwards said he saw no reason for obtruding these facts, since, evening after evening, the cousins resolved themselves into a committee of ways and means upon the problem, and always preferred to accept the benevolent interference of the godmother, who was superior to any difficulties of time and space, and had no further use for articles that are no part of spiritual furniture.

"True, the intention was balked of its completeness by the absence of the other ear-ring, but one should not be too avaricious in dealing with the Immortals. Content with what they give is the condition of the process, and the story of the three wishes by which the peasant and his wife found themselves, after all, no better off than before, is a lesson in prayer not to be forgotten.

"So the girls waited, in the patience of true faith, for the fulfillment of the business, and they were rewarded, even beyond their expectations, and, as is the celestial manner, on a wholly different scale, which is the weak point of the drama of Job, where sheep, oxen, camels, sons and daughters are taken away to be replaced, apparently to the satisfaction of the patriarch, by more sheep, more oxen, more camels, more sons and more daughters.

"But if James die, doth George replace him? David knew better when he said, 'Oh, Absalom, my son Absalom, would God I had died for thee, oh, Absalom, my son.'

"The earring then on one side is clearly traced to pew 31 and Miss Jane from pew 33 to Palafox Park, where, the same day, the ornament is subsequently found, conveyed thither in some hospitable fold of the wrapping that received it on its detachment from Cousin Cornelia's ear.

"Naturally at this point ends the story."

"I have my doubts," said the Major, "about this last

part of the business, the carriage of the earring to Pala-fox Park."

"Well," replied the madam, "as to the probabilities of that I am willing they should be tested by the results of an accident with which you are all familiar. Did you, Major, ever lose a collar-button?"

"Certainly—not a week ago."

"Where did you find it?"

"It was—let me see—" Here the Major was suddenly seized with a violent fit of coughing. He was vigorously thumped on the back in that insane way people have when certain something must be done and ignorant of exactly what to do.

In great seeming distress the Major rushed from the room, and in a few minutes thereafter could have been seen with the Colonel, still quite red in the face, but re-lieved in mind, and placidly smoking a Reina Victoria.

"I wonder what did become of the collar-button," muttered the Assistant-Surgeon.

But nobody ever knew, except the Major's man, who discovered it where it was never designed to be; but, as was said of Vespasian's silver, recovered from a similar local-ity, *non olet*.

"Perhaps," interposed the madam, "some other gen-tleman has doubts——"

"Certainly I could have none after my experience," replied one of the younger captains. "I was struggling with my collar-button the other morning when it sud-denly slipped out of my fingers and disappeared.

"I hunted everywhere, the more earnestly since I had no other, and was dressing against time for the early train to town. At last I had to content myself with a pin, which narrowly missed the jugular, as I wickedly thrust it into my shirt.

"But that was only a beginning of misery. My foot pained me all day long, and spoilt a trip among the book-stores to which I had been looking forward for a month, and saving up enough for the especial purpose of securing a two volume edition of Gen. Henry Lee's Memoirs, with notes on the margin, written, as I had reason to suppose, by General Sumter.

"That evening when I reached home without my prize, which had been disposed of just a moment before I hobbled into the place, I unearthed the missing button from the toe of my boot.

"I keep a card of them now stuck into the looking-glass."

"It would seem," added the madam, "that buttons may be as evasive as earrings."

"I feel," interrupted one of the senior lieutenants, "I feel as though I ought to contribute a remark or two on this occasion. Like the saint who carried his own head, so with the woman who unconsciously became the possessor of her neighbor's earring, it is only the first step that makes the trouble. Once at large, these trinkets are amenable neither to law nor logic. I have my doubts about guardian angels, but am clear as to the existence of imps of depravity charged to try the tempers of men. The toilet and the desk are their favorite fields of operation. Not a pin, for instance, can be found on the cushion, but a trip in bare feet over the floor detects any number of them.

"A memorandum suddenly disappears that you know you have seen but a moment before. The hunt for it wastes a half-hour, and, after an explosion that gives the devil a safe mortgage upon your soul, behold! the memorandum appears right before you, looking more innocent than a rose-bud.

"I, too, have a collar-button, only one incident in the history of which I will give this afternoon. It vanished when under process of adjustment, and there was nothing to do but find it, unless I remained in bed, which was impossible, for it was the last of the month, with muster and inspection pending, as well as a visit to the paymaster and a subsequent lunch with my *compadre*.

"I am frequently complimented on my good nature and sagacity, and I felt these were both at stake, and resolved to be firm and circumspect. The first thing to do was to undress and examine carefully each article of my clothing, which I did, pleasantly humming to myself: 'We may be happy yet.'

"It was useless, so I turned to the bed and took off spread, blanket and sheet, and deposited them in the middle of the floor, still continuing the old familiar strain.

"Then I closely examined the six sides of the mattress, not forgetting the corners nor the melody.

"Giving my attention to the lighter articles of furniture in the vicinity, I piled them up, after examination, upon the mattress. Drawing my sword, I began to rake under the heavier pieces, but I was too tired to sing and out on the parade I could hear muster in progress.

"My temper threatened to rise, and I felt that I must rely upon bodily exercise to keep down spiritual rebellion, so I struck up,

> "'Oh, won't it be joyful, joyful, joyful,
> When we meet to part no more,'

and commenced to kick the smaller impediments about the room.

"Just here the door opened and my wife appeared.

"'Edwin, oh, Edwin,' she shrieked, and rushed downstairs to send for the Doctor. Circumstances seemed to be passing beyond my control. I stuck my sword into the mattress, wrapped myself up in some of the drapery and sat down on the washstand. I ought to state here that I am troubled with *hyperæsthesia*, and my wife knew that at this time I was living mainly upon hot water in the morning and sage tea at night.

"Pretty soon I saw her peering anxiously over the banisters and I remarked in my mildest manner, 'Putting aside any incompleteness in the way of wardrobe, my dear Isabella, I may truthfully state that I am glad to see you.'

"'Edwin, what is the matter!'

"'Rest assured I am neither mad nor drunk. I have lost my collar-button, and am trying to find it.'

"The door-bell rang and my wife went down to dispose of the Doctor. She said she had an intermittent headache, acute pain at brief intervals over the left eyebrow. The Doctor advised spectacles and diet, with a cessation of all literary labor, which was a shrewd inference on his part, from the contents of the table, consisting of a cook-book, upon—ah—'How to make bread,' and an order for Lord & Taylor, which the Doctor evidently mistook for the manuscript of a novel.

"He promised to send over a lotion for topical application, which he did, and my wife presented it to the cook, who was always having 'miseries,' and who always felt better after a little medicine.

"When my wife came back I was putting things to rights. She loaned me her collar-button and I went over to explain my absence to the commanding officer. He was very grave at first, but the moment I mentioned my accident he broke down completely. 'That will do,' said he; 'don't say any more. I have been there myself.'

"Late the next day, happening to be in the metropolis, I felt thirsty and went into Stewart's to get a glass of iced milk. I knew I had some small change in my pocket and pulled out a handful of the contents to get a quarter, and there among keys, dimes and sea-beans—there, conspicuously on top of everything, was my collar-button. That is all I have to say.'"

"May I ask a question?"

This came from a lieutenant who, by virtue of frequent detail as judge advocate, had acquired a chronic interrogative attitude.

"Certainly."

"Between the morning of your adventure and the time of the iced—milk, had you not changed your dress?"

"Of course."

"And you have no explanations to offer as to the behavior of the collar-button in this transfer?"

"Oh, yes; it was maliciously at the bottom of everything then."

"One moment, if you please," said the Assistant-Surgeon. "If I heard rightly, you mentioned *sea beans* as part of the produce of your pocket."

"I did."

"I wish I understood why anybody should burden himself with such things."

"As a sure specific against rheumatism."

"Is it possible you can believe that."

"All I know is that since I carried them, I have never had an attack."

But the Assistant was not an adept in cross-examination.

"Your experience, gentlemen," interposed the madam, "will, I think, convince you that there was nothing improbable in the undesigned carriage of the ear-rings from St. Thomas-by-the-sea to Palafox Park."

The Judge Advocate, whose forehead ran back into his occiput like a glacier bisecting an Alpine slope, still succeeded in maintaining as strong an appearance of judicial dubiety as Lord Eldon's wig itself.

Then the Colonel's wife slowly unwound from her head the scarf which at the beginning of our story had attracted the kind intervention of the Quartermaster, and aroused the suspicions of the Assistant-Surgeon. He watched the operation, and thought, "She still has a pretty arm, and likes to show it."

But the Judge-Advocate saw something more. Slowly he rose and with a profound bow said, "Madam, I, too, am a believer."

And the Senior Lieutenant cried out, "Why, these are the very earrings themselves."

And it was so.

But the Assistant-Surgeon, finding he was equally wrong in both remarks and conjectures, went home and resolved hereafter to secure entire freedom from all emotion or desire and spend the rest of his life like the monks of Mount Athos in the search of perfection by contemplating the pit of his stomach.

"Madam, before we go I would like a little information on one point."

This was the Chaplain, who, practiced in thinking by subdivisions up as high as fifteenthly, was better enabled than most to keep a firm hold upon any verbal meandering.

"I judge from something said in the early part of your most agreeable continuation of the Colonel's story, that there is a hiatus, so to speak, in the genealogy of these earrings. Is it not so?"

"I'll tell you next Christmas."

" Gentle breath of yours my sails
Must fill, or else my project fails,
Which was to please."

Tempest.

"*Falstaff.* Have you provided me here half a dozen sufficient men ?
Shallow. Marry have we, sir,
Falstaff. Let me see them, I beseech you.
Shallow. Where's the roll ? where's the roll ?
. . . . Let them appear as I call."

Shakespeare.

LIST OF CONTRIBUTORS: